Praise for

N̂

Well written and insanel̲   ̲c̲ of the things I
liked best about this booᴋ ̲as the way Cartwright
had of explaining the BDSM lifestyle... I'm definitely
looking forward to the next installment in this
Mastered series and will be rereading With This Collar
while I wait, for it is a great scorching love story well
worth reading at any time. ~ *Whipped Cream*

This very spicy read gives a beautiful exposition of
one woman's journey into an erotic world that she
knew very little of... There are very hot scenes that
demonstrate some of the techniques that can be
applied but this is also a delicious love story and I
look forward to reading more titles from this gifted
author. ~ *Night Owl Romance*

Ms. Cartwright managed to deliver yet another
amazing BDSM story. I enjoyed reading With this
Collar immensely. It is well written and perfectly
paced. The characters are great—even the side ones
that I can't wait to read more about—and there are
just enough witty lines to highlight the sassy part of
their personalities... Can't wait to read more.
~ *The Romance Reviews*

With This Collar by Sierra Cartwright is a beautifully
written BDSM story that contains the heart and soul of
the BDSM world. Ms. Cartwright did not miss a beat
in creating Master Marcus and Julia... As far as the
plot goes, this is a rock solid read that will heat you up
in a Nano second! The characters demand your

attention as the story unfolds. I enjoyed the fact that Julia fights back. What can I say…I like a woman with gumption. Ms. Cartwright is a master in her own right when it comes to writing the BDSM genre. She gets an A++ from me. With This Collar is a must have for anyone's BDSM collection. Bring on the next book in the series! ~ *BlackRaven's Reviews*

Sierra Cartwright never fails to wow me, no matter what the story. On His Terms grabbed me by the hair on the first page and didn't let up. How do you even go into a party wanting to be trained by one Dom only to be intended for another. This book is a sexy romp through what it means to be in a BDSM relationship, from some of the most basic submissive actions, like getting cake and serving it without falling over to learning in great detail what it means to submit. I loved the development of this story as it began with Chelsea as a hungry media vixen and how she morphed into a woman who begins to love the Dom she was just using to get to where she wanted to go. Will he feel the same? I'll never tell, but this series is one you are going to want to have in your e-reader if you love BDSM stories. ~ *Erzabet's Enchantments*

I really enjoyed Sydney Wallace. She's intelligent, saucy and has just enough baggage to be multi-dimensional. Michael is intense, patient and solid…just what Sydney needs. The pace was brisk enough, and the sex was spicy and molten… Over the Line is a delicious erotic read for all fans of BDSM.
~ *Fallen Angel Reviews*

Total-E-Bound Publishing books by Sierra Cartwright:

Mastered
With This Collar
On His Terms
Over the Line

Signed, Sealed & Delivered
Bound and Determined
Her Two Doms

Anthologies
Naughty Nibbles: This Time
Naughty Nibbles: Fed Up
Bound Brits: S&M 101
Subspace: Three-way Tie
Night of the Senses: Voyeur
Bound to the Billionaire: Bared to Him

Seasonal Collections
Halloween Hearthrobs: Walk on the Wild Side
Homecoming: Unbound Surrender

Clasndestine Classics
Jane Eyre

Mastered

IN HIS CUFFS

SIERRA CARTWRIGHT

IN HIS CUFFS

Dedication

For one of the most brilliant women I have ever known: Claire Siemaszkiewicz. You are my heroine!

Chapter One

Finally.

She'd made it.

Maggie smoothed the front of her short leather skirt and followed her friend Vanessa through the front door of the Den.

Music blasted from the back patio and the bass seemed to shake the walls. Half-naked people — men, mostly — were everywhere, and cool air whispered in through open windows.

Gregorio, the Den's caretaker, met them in the foyer.

"Welcome to Ladies' Night," he said. His eyes were dark, and the wink of a silver earring made him resemble a pirate.

"I'm here for the debauchery," Maggie said.

"You've come to the right place," he assured her with a grin.

She'd been looking forward to this outing for over a month. Not only had she spent her lunch hours shopping online for a new outfit and killer shoes, but she'd also purchased a sparkly collar. Every day at five o'clock, she happily slashed through the date on her calendar. The fat, red mark served a dual purpose. It served as a reward for surviving another workday with the insufferable David Tomlinson, and it was a visual reminder that she was closer to a night at the Den, where she would satisfy her deepest cravings.

"Are you planning to scene tonight, Maggie?" Gregorio asked.

She nodded.

"Sex?"

"I won't say no," she said.

"Condoms are provided in all the private rooms. House Monitors also have them. I take it you want to participate as a sub, not a Domme?"

"That's correct." She wondered how he managed to keep up with the particulars of each guest. But then, that was why he ran the place.

"Are you looking to play with a man or a woman?"

"Strictly het," she said.

Several different coloured wristbands lay on a nearby table. Gregorio selected a white one and affixed it to her wrist.

"Switches are in yellow," he continued.

"That's the one I want," Vanessa chimed in.

"Seriously?" Maggie asked.

Vanessa shrugged. "You never know what opportunities might present themselves."

"As always, Dominants have red bands," Gregorio said.

"Got it." Maggie was anxious to start the festivities. She'd been here often enough that she could take Gregorio's place at the door. But she also knew he wouldn't hurry through the ritual, despite her impatience.

"House Monitors have black bands around their upper arms. House subs have purple ones. Be sure to let someone know if you need help. The Den's safe word is 'halt', use it at any time. Enjoy yourselves."

"I will, for sure," Vanessa said.

Brandy, a woman Maggie knew as a house sub, took their jackets and purses.

Any night here was fabulous, but four times a year, Master Damien and Gregorio went all out for the house's single ladies, providing entertainment, demonstrations, Doms and Dommes, exotic non-alcoholic beverages and the most mouthwatering desserts imaginable. She'd been saving up her calories for over a week with the intention of indulging in all her favourite things. Not that it mattered, really. If she had her way, she'd burn plenty of energy during a BDSM scene or two.

To her, an orgasm was the best of all stress-relievers. And a dozen would make her forget the crappy hell her life had become.

With luck, it would take less than half an hour to find someone to take her to the downstairs dungeon.

She and Vanessa made their way towards the kitchen and looked out of the patio doors. A fire burned in a pit. People in all sorts of outfits, from street clothes to club wear, milled about. A stage had been set up near the back of the paved area where rocker Evan C all but made love to the microphone.

"I'll have a double shot of that deliciousness," Vanessa said against Maggie's ear.

"Evan C?" The musician oozed sex appeal. Tonight he wore an unbuttoned black shirt, and, as always, his trademark white scarf was wrapped around his neck. A recent video of him had gone viral, thanks to a publicity stunt by one of the Den's members. So now Evan C was giving women all over the world heart palpitations.

"I'd let him put his scarf over my headboard," Vanessa said. "But no, I mean the guy standing to the right of the stage. I think he has on a black band."

Since the party attracted so many newbies, Master Damien brought in extra House Monitors—male and female—to ensure everyone's safety, answer questions and even participate in scenes. "I don't know who you're talking about." Her platform shoes added much-needed inches, but that didn't help her see through the crowd any better.

"The man over there." Vanessa pointed. "Near the speaker. Short dark hair. Jeans. No shirt. Can you see him yet?"

"No."

"Wait. I think that's a pair of handcuffs on his belt loop. Damn."

Maggie craned her head.

"Do you need me to lift you up?"

She glared at Vanessa. Vanessa was five inches taller than Maggie and never missed an opportunity to point that out.

"Would you care for a chocolate-covered strawberry?" a server enquired, distracting them.

"Oh, God, yes," Maggie said.

Vanessa and Maggie both turned away from the huge glass windows and towards the hot man standing near them. He was over six feet tall, with long hair she itched to run her fingers through.

She took her time selecting a treat from the silver serving platter. If nothing else, she enjoyed keeping him next to her for an extra few seconds. Not only did he smell of expensive, spicy cologne, but he had on a bow tie and remarkable, shimmery gold pants. His chest was devoid of hair, and his skin glistened as if oiled. Master Damien *definitely* knew how to please his guests.

She chose a strawberry with the most chocolate coating, while Vanessa, in typical fashion, dived in after the biggest piece of fruit.

Where Maggie was deliberate, Vanessa seized every opportunity that came along. The fact they were so different had made the friendship all sorts of interesting over the last eight years. Maggie nibbled at her dessert while Vanessa bit hers in half.

"Another, ladies?" the man offered.

"Could you leave the tray?" Vanessa asked.

"Don't you dare," Maggie countered.

Vanessa picked up two more berries, but Maggie shook her head. The man winked at Maggie before moving off.

"The sexy man I was looking at earlier is gone. You never saw him, did you?"

"Not like it's a loss. There's plenty of them here."

"True enough. But I like handcuffs. So do you, right?"

Maggie nodded. She loved any kind of restraint.

"So, have you seen anyone you're interested in?" Vanessa asked.

After she'd eaten her strawberry, Maggie surveyed the crowd in the kitchen and great room. "I wouldn't mind sceneing with the HM I played with last time, if he's here. He knew his way around my body without a map." The man had flogged her good then sank to his knees and licked her pussy until she couldn't come anymore. "How about you?"

"I'm greedy. I want two men."

"Two?" Maggie hadn't considered trying a ménage, but now...

"It *is* Ladies' Night," Vanessa pointed out.

"So it is."

The music trailed off and enthusiastic applause followed. She wiped her hands on a paper cocktail napkin then joined in.

A few seconds later, Evan C introduced his next song — the single that was accelerating up the charts — then nodded to his band who cranked up the sound.

"Got your kink on?" Vanessa asked.

"Almost." Nerves assailed her, a heady combination of adrenaline and expectation.

They made plans to meet up later at their hotel room in Winter Park. Master Damien had thoughtfully provided a shuttle between the Den and several stops in the nearby tourist town. "If you go home with anyone, send me a text," Maggie said.

"Same for you."

"Yeah. As if."

"Hey, you could shock the world and do something totally out of character."

Maggie rolled her eyes. Ever since her breakup with Samuel, she'd been in a sexual drought. Then again, it had been all but barren while they were together. He'd tried, at least at first. But after several months, he'd got angry with her.

During one of their arguments, he'd shouted that she was insatiable. That wasn't true. She would have been fine if he'd ever tied her to the bed and used her vibrator on her. A spanking once a week would have satisfied her needs. Well...at least she thought it would have. If it was hard enough, the after-effects would remind her of the pain, then the anticipation would have carried her through the remaining days.

Then again, perhaps the more she got, the more she'd want.

But she might not ever know.

She'd never had a relationship that had made it past six months. If she found a man who was demanding in the bedroom, he tended to be an arrogant son of a bitch outside it. If he was considerate about sharing chores, he tended to bore her once the lights were turned down. And two men had insisted it wasn't right to hit a woman. More than once she'd tried to explain the difference between a consensual spanking and striking out in anger. Her words had fallen on deaf ears.

Recently, she'd cancelled all her dating site memberships. She'd given up searching for Mr Right and decided to settle for Mr Right Now.

Because of that, she lived for her forays to the Den, where her desires were encouraged.

She'd learnt to embrace her single status. She didn't have to answer to anyone if she worked late. If she didn't feel like getting out of her pyjamas on a Saturday morning she didn't have to. She could eat ice cream for dinner or skip vacuuming for so long that dust bunnies threatened to strangle her.

And she could play with different Doms all the time. The exhilaration of not knowing what to expect added to her delirium.

"Targets acquired," Vanessa said over her shoulder as she headed towards a group of men in the great room.

Maggie snagged a virgin pina colada from the granite island in the kitchen then joined the crowd on the patio.

She stood to one side and watched a few couples dance in front of the stage. Off to the left, a tall, broad male knelt in front of a woman who wore a red wristband. The image was erotic, but it didn't do much for her. When she was here, she preferred giving up control. At work, she engaged in constant battles with her self-appointed boss and had to be on guard all the time. Letting go and surrendering to her submissive tendencies was critical to her mental health.

"Would you like to dance?"

She turned and smiled at the man who'd approached her. He was tall and lanky, wearing a plaid shirt. At least he'd skipped the pocket protector.

Part of her knew she was being unfair. He had an earnest smile, and she was sure he was a nice man. He had on a red band, but somehow, she didn't see him as a Dom. There was something lacking in his tone, a certain confidence. And his expression was more hopeful than assertive.

She smiled back and waited a few seconds. He continued to look at her, but she had no compulsion to cast her gaze at the ground. She felt no spark of attraction for him. If she was going to bare her body — or at least parts of it — to a stranger, she would choose a man who had a razor-edge of danger about him. For some reason, this guy reminded her of her of Samuel. She couldn't imagine a greater turn-off. "Thanks," she said. "Perhaps another time."

"It was worth a try," he said easily before moving onto the next possibility, a woman who was swaying as she listened to Evan C.

In some ways, Maggie realised, this wasn't much different than a singles' bar. But there were far fewer pretensions. At least sexually.

Maggie took a sip from the cool drink, loving the blend of pineapple, coconut and whipped cream on her tongue. Since it had juice in it, she told herself the beverage was at least somewhat healthy.

She was ready to take a second sip when she saw him.

David Tomlinson.

Her nemesis.

What the hell was he doing here?

Slowly, she lowered her trembling hand.

Fuck.

The main reason she'd come to the Den was to escape him.

He stood near a speaker, arms folded across his bare chest, a black band on his upper arm, short hair spiked, and he was wearing a pair of jeans.

David Tomlinson was a House Monitor? Crap. It wasn't enough that he was here, but he had to have a role of authority.

Then she noticed the handcuffs.

She gawked at the sight.

Was David Tomlinson the man Vanessa had noticed?

If Maggie didn't know him so well, she might agree that he was sexy. But she knew him too well. He manipulated people to his own ends. Sure, he was one of the smartest people she'd ever met, but she'd seen him use that intelligence for nefarious purposes.

She stood there, uncertain what to do. Confront him? Ignore him and hope he didn't see her? Catch the shuttle back to Winter Park?

Immediately, she dismissed the last idea.

She was here to have a good time, and by God, she would enjoy herself.

Ignoring him wasn't her normal style. No way would she spend the entire night skulking around and looking over her shoulder.

That left a confrontation, and really, the only thing that suited her personality.

As if sensing her gaze, he looked at her.

He scowled—a ferocious expression that was all-too familiar. Obviously he was as surprised and as unhappy to see her as she was to see him. Then a sub walked up to him, and he turned his attention to the blonde.

Maggie exhaled a breath she hadn't realised she'd sucked in.

She took another sip of her drink, trying to regroup. She told herself they were both adults. They were both here for their own reasons. They could deal with this.

Determinedly, she went inside and wandered around the living room. A small group was gathered near the fireplace, and the topic of conversation was the Denver Broncos' upcoming preseason schedule.

Near the window, a Dom rested his shoulders on the wall.

Though he wasn't overly tall, he was broad. He had on a T-shirt, revealing his beefy biceps. He could probably wield a flogger for a good long time.

He glanced pointedly at her wrist then back at her.

Her heart rate increased and she tightened her grip on her virgin pina colada. She cast her gaze at the ground, silently signalling both her submissiveness and willingness.

When she raised her head, she was shocked to see him striding away from her, out of the room.

"If you want someone to scene with, I'll take care of you."

The voice froze her from the inside out. Since she heard it all day, every day, she recognised it instantly. Rich and deep, as controlled as it was reviled.

When her heart started to beat again, she swung to face her adversary. She looked a long way up into his deep, dark blue, unfathomable eyes.

His jaw was set, and his arms were folded across his chest.

"Damn you." She scowled. "Did you make him go away?"

"Yes."

"What the hell is wrong with you? Isn't it enough that you ruin every one of my days?"

"I've always wanted to have you over my lap for the good spanking you deserve."

She blinked, for once shocked into silence by his words. Since they'd met, he'd been standoffish. Business was the only thing they'd ever discussed. And he'd harboured thoughts of having his hand on her ass?

"Maybe we should satisfy our mutual desires."

"Not in this lifetime, David."

"Tonight even," he countered.

She laughed, hoping it didn't sound as brittle as it felt. "Even for you, that's an arrogant statement."

"I spent the last few minutes watching your reflection in the glass, Margaret—"

"Maggie," she corrected through gritted teeth.

"Not only do you have on a white wristband," he continued as if she hadn't spoken, "but you lowered your gaze for that Dom."

Her stomach executed a somersault. "Do you know how to mind your own business? Ever?"

"I pay attention to detail."

"There's an understatement." During the first three weeks that he'd taken control of her family's firm, he'd looked at every piece of paper, analysed spreadsheets, sat down with each employee in private, insisted on meeting all of their vendors and reviewed all current customer files. At this point, it seemed he knew as much about World Wide Now as she did.

"For example, I know you're flustered," he continued.

"So you're a psychic in addition to having superior business acumen?" If sarcasm were arsenic, he'd be dead.

"You're thinking about lifting your skirt for me and lowering yourself over my lap. You're wondering if I'll hit you as hard as you need."

"That's insane," she insisted, but now that he'd mentioned it, she couldn't help picturing that very thing.

"You're hoping I'll let you keep your underwear on. And yes, you are wearing panties."

She blinked, stunned. How the hell could he know that?

"If you were as calm as you'd like me to believe, you wouldn't be stabbing the bottom of your glass with your straw."

She froze, not realising she had been betraying her inner turmoil.

This David confounded her.

In typical fashion, his dark hair was spiked and brushed severely back from his broad forehead. His eyebrows were drawn together in an arrogant, masculine slash.

As she'd noticed earlier, he wore a pair of dark denim jeans, but she hadn't seen the scuffed, black motorcycle boots.

Except for his trademark arrogance, he didn't resemble the man she knew from work.

Normally he wore expensive power suits with crisp button-down shirts. The only concession to an occasional casual look was a loosened knot in his requisite red or blue tie.

She'd spent so much time being irritated by him that she'd never really noticed him as a man.

But now…

His shoulders were broad and his waist trim. The black HM band emphasised the size of his arms. Clearly he had a gym membership, and he used it.

David's jeans showed off the size of his thighs in a way dress slacks never could. Heaven help her, she couldn't help but stare at the thick black belt encircling his waist. Add in the cuffs that refracted the overhead light… He made breathing difficult.

"How about it, Maggie?"

She looked up at him. His use of Maggie rather than Margaret had been intentional, as if he knew exactly the effect it would have on her. She would never scene with a man who didn't respect her wishes, and he was proving he would. "What happened to your no fraternising policy?"

Several more people entered the room, and the noise level increased. He took hold of her shoulders and moved her backwards. She didn't protest. How could she with the way oxygen deprivation was suddenly making it impossible to think?

He released his grip, but he'd effectively trapped her in a corner, her back to the wall. The act seemed symbolic of their entire relationship. He was adept at manoeuvring her to suit his wishes.

Six months ago, when he'd decided to acquire World Wide Now for far less money than Maggie believed it was worth, she'd put up a fiery verbal protest. Rather than deal with her directly, David had taken her mother aside.

He'd told Gloria that Maggie's retention was critical to the success of the firm.

In a brilliant strategic move, he'd then called Maggie back into a private meeting and presented a deal that gave him everything he wanted.

If they met his lofty goals, meaning Maggie worked her ass off and brought in sales, her mother would be rewarded with half a million dollars at the end of two years. He hadn't promised Maggie a penny beyond her regular wages, but he'd somehow figured that taking care of her mother was the biggest incentive of all for Maggie.

Her mother had told Maggie she didn't have to accept his terms. Another deal, perhaps a better one, would come along. Together, they'd figure it out.

But once David had shown her the reality of World Wide Now's fiscal picture due to her mother's mismanagement, Maggie had seen no other option. She loved her mother and wanted her to have freedom from the financial struggles she'd always endured.

If he had simply waltzed in as lord and master, Maggie would have flipped him the bird on the way out of the door. But he was far too smart for that. Still, that didn't mean she liked or appreciated his manipulation.

Once she'd nodded, he'd pulled out an employment contract. The bastard had prepared it ahead of time. She had signed her name with short, angry strokes. In corporate speak, she was shackled in golden handcuffs.

And that wasn't much different from the metal pair dangling from his belt loop. Despite her resolve, she kept glancing at them.

He took the glass from her hand and gave it to a passing waiter.

She felt no fear as he leaned towards her, crowding her space. They breathed the same air, and his scent intoxicated her—power, spiced with raw masculine confidence.

"I think we can both agree this is an exception. You wouldn't be doing this to get ahead at work. I wouldn't be forcing you to do it to keep your job. At the office, we'll have the same arrangement we have now," he told her.

"Meaning you'll set my schedule, tell me what to do, organise my life, prioritise my tasks and I'll agree with you."

"Much the same way as it'll be tonight, yes." His smile was predatory.

She shuddered then regretted she'd allowed him the glimpse of her vulnerability. "I have no intention of sceneing with you," she said.

"The choice is always yours. Do you know the club's safe word?" he asked her.

She blinked. "We're not having this conversation."

"Do you know the safe word?" he repeated.

"Of course."

"Then tell me what it is."

She felt as if she was involved in a game whose rules she didn't understand. "Halt."

"If you want me to walk away, say it."

Awareness of him simmered in her, its effects causing a slow heating of her blood. One word would end their discussion. That's what she should want. So why was she still here, feeling tempted? "You don't play fair."

"I like to win," he agreed. His plainly stated words took away any further argument. "You and I both know that in any D/s relationship, the sub has the real power. You get to set the rules and the pace. If I don't agree to your terms, we have no deal." He paused. "In a way, the tables are turned. It seems to me you should relish that after six months."

"It won't be your butt that's being blistered."

"Or legs," he added. "Or shoulders. Or breasts." He leaned in a fraction of an inch closer.

It stunned her how threatened, how on fire she suddenly felt. He'd barely moved, but she was snared.

"Or pussy," he said finally.

She pressed herself harder against the wall, needing its support. "I'm not saying I would ever agree to your insane suggestion..."

"Go on."

"If I did, we wouldn't talk about it at the office."

"What happens here, stays here. It will change nothing about our dynamic at the office, if that's what you're afraid of."

"I'm not afraid of anything, David," she said, her words infused with bravado she was sure he could see through.

Maggie reminded herself she didn't like him. But damn, there was something about his commanding manner that intrigued her. Every day, she watched him in action. When he wanted something, he pursued it with single-minded determination. A very feminine part of her wondered what it would feel like to be the focus of that attention.

"Do you have your own safe word that you prefer?"

"Halt is fine."

"How about a word to slow things down?"

"Eclipse."

He tilted his head to the side.

"I'm more likely to say accelerate," she told him.

"I wouldn't have figured you for an extreme player."

"You think you're a sage, Mr Tomlinson," she said. "But you've misread a few things about me."

"I'll give you that. From the way you behave at the office, I would have taken you for a Domme."

"It might be fun to strap you to a St Andrew's cross," she said, raising one of her waxed eyebrows.

He laughed.

She blinked. During the time she'd known him, she had never heard him laugh. She'd rarely even seen him smile. Was it possible she'd judged him too harshly? Then she recalled the way he'd even provided the ballpoint pen for her to sign the hated employment agreement. "I'll take that as a no, then."

"Not a chance in hell," he affirmed. "The only one feeling a lash will be you. And feel it you will."

Before she could respond to his flat, arrogant statement, he continued, "I assure you I will be very observant about your reactions." He captured her chin and tipped her head back. "I want to know what quickens your pulse. I'll find out what dampens your panties. I want to know all of your erotic sounds and what each means."

She wished she had met him here first, that she'd seen him as an exciting Dom, felt the connection and agreed to scene. But she couldn't pretend their relationship wasn't already laden with hostility and distrust.

"For tonight," he reminded her. "Just tonight. Say yes, Maggie mine."

If she was smart, she'd tell him no. She shouldn't want this, him. But every nerve ending zinged. Desire won the battle over common sense. "Yes." She nodded.

Desire seemed to flare in his eyes, widening them. "Good," he said.

He released her and stepped back.

She was grateful for the physical space. This close, she noticed how male he was, sexy, sensual and threatening.

"Any hard limits?" he asked.

This part of a negotiation was familiar, and she relaxed into it. She was good at asking for what she wanted. "No blood, edgeplay, permanent marks."

"How about formal protocols?"

She'd had enough experience to know that Doms differed on what that meant. But in this setting, since they weren't a couple, she doubted he would ask for anything she'd find objectionable. "If it suits you, I'm okay with it."

"We'll observe some, but I don't require strict adherence. I want you to communicate."

She nodded.

"What are your limits around humiliation?"

"As long as I'm not left alone for long periods, I'm fine."

"I won't leave you alone, ever. If you're suffering for me, I want to watch and enjoy every moment of it."

There was something about the huskiness in his voice—part promise, part threat—that made her tremble. She looked at him. The set of his jaw emphasised the seriousness of his words.

Maggie would have never suspected she'd willingly experience anguish for David Tomlinson, even offer herself to him, but in this moment, there was nothing she wanted more.

"And suffer you will, Maggie," he promised.

Chapter Two

Maggie froze as David reached forward to tuck a few stray strands of hair behind her ear.

His gesture was tender, a contradiction to what she knew lay ahead.

"Your wristband indicates you're open to having sex, but given the nature of our relationship, I think we should discuss it." He lowered his hand to trace a finger around the top of her collar.

Goosebumps ran up her arms. His touch was a distraction, and his question loomed large. She considered her answer.

She'd have to face him on Monday morning and every day for over a year. Maggie hated awkward emotional entanglements, so she'd never slept with anyone she worked with. She also knew she could compartmentalise with the best of them. "We're both adults," she said. "If the scene leads to sex, and it feels like a natural progression, I'm sure there won't be any repercussions."

"I want to be very clear about this." He slid his finger beneath the collar. "You're open to it?"

"Yes." She nodded.

"I can fuck you as hard and as long as I want?"

The words, so raw, natural, caught her off guard. "I thought you were a House Monitor. Don't you have things you need to do?"

"I'm off duty for the next two hours."

"Master Damien agreed to that?"

"I asked for three. We compromised at two." With his fingertip, he drew her a little closer.

"Pretty sure of yourself," she said. "No one can sustain a scene for that long."

"We're wasting time. Anything else you want to discuss before I take you downstairs?"

"Ah..." The moment was here. It was real. And she really had no doubts. "I'm good."

He waited a few seconds before nodding. "In that case, let's get to my rules."

Maggie laughed a little. "I knew there was a catch."

"You're comfortable calling me Mr Tomlinson, you can use that in addition to Sir."

She scowled. She used Mr Tomlinson to drive distance between them, not as a term of respect. Calling him that would alter their dynamic. "Well played," she said.

"Any objections to that?"

"No."

"I expect straightforward communication and honest answers to any questions I ask."

"Sounds fair."

"If you're ready, I think it's about time to get on with it."

She nodded.

"Please respond verbally."

"Yes."

"Yes, what?" he prompted.

"Yes, Mr Tomlinson."

He looked over his shoulder and signalled to Brandy. The sub moved towards them, and he released his hold on Maggie's collar. Instead of letting her go, he rested his fingertips on her shoulder. She felt the warmth and firmness of his touch even through the fabric of her shirt.

She appreciated that he hadn't let go of her completely. She'd said she didn't like to be left alone for extended periods, and he seemed to have extrapolated from there, figuring she liked constant assurance from her Dom.

Until now, she hadn't realised how nice that was.

"Please fetch me a leash," he said when Brandy joined them. "And my personal bag was checked when I arrived. Brown leather. I'd like that as well."

"Of course, Master David."

Maggie had never been leashed. She'd bought the sparkly, hot-pink leather strip for show. She hadn't anticipated it would actually be used as a collar.

Within a minute, the blonde sub returned. With her head bowed, she extended the items he'd requested.

David thanked the woman. He placed the toy bag on the floor then accepted the black nylon lead.

With a quick curtsey, Brandy left them.

Maggie's gaze was fixated on the lead. His motions were quick and efficient as he attached it in place.

"I'll expect you to keep the tension taut so that you keep the appropriate distance between us," he told her. "Please keep your hands behind your back, except for when we are on the stairs. Your safety matters, so I want you to hold onto the banister. Do you have any problems with my instructions?"

"No...Mr Tomlinson." Damn, the formality of the address, especially minus her implied sarcasm, sounded odd. But she was sure it had his desired effect. They were Dom and sub, not co-workers, not friends.

"Say that again, please," he instructed.

He'd spoken softly, but with a steel undertone. With her, it was far, far more effective than if he'd been harsh. She looked at him. Her heart rate decreased as she began to slip into a submissive mindset. "I understand your instructions, Mr Tomlinson, and I have no problem with them."

"Very good."

His approval made her relax her shoulders.

"You look very pretty on my leash, Maggie."

"I... Thank you, Mr Tomlinson." Resisting the urge to tug on the hem of her skirt and cover herself, she laced her hands at the small of her back.

He wrapped the length of nylon around his hand twice, obviously planning to keep her close. "Ready?"

"Yes, Mr Tomlinson."

With a brief nod, he turned and began to walk.

It took her a couple of steps to match his pace and get accustomed to being led. No one paid attention to them as they moved through the main level of the luxurious mountain retreat.

At the top of the stairs, he gave the leash some slack. He descended slowly, and she appreciated his thoughtfulness.

The main room of the house's dungeon also had a number of people gathered around. A kneeling sub was attached to a ring on the wall. A couple waited for beverages in front of the bar, and servers moved through the space, carrying bottles of water and more trays filled with delicacies.

Master Damien walked over to talk to them. "I see Maggie has agreed to play with you."

The house owner looked at her, rather than David. She knew Master Damien was checking on her, giving her an out. "I did, Sir," she told him.

"He'll make you cry," Master Damien warned.

She hazarded a quick glance at her Dom for the evening.

David shrugged. "It has happened once or twice."

"As you know, Sir," she said to Master Damien, "I don't cry."

"I'm afraid you might have just issued a challenge," Master Damien said with a quick grin.

This man was an enigma to her. Although she saw him every time she came to the Den, she knew very little about him. Sometimes he wore a suit, other times he was much more casual in jeans and a T-shirt. Tonight he wore slacks and a black lightweight sweater.

On occasion, she'd seen him with his hair pulled back and secured with a thin strip of leather. Tonight it was loose, with the ends curled against his collar.

Rumours about him were rampant. The only thing people were pretty sure about was the fact he lived in seclusion. She'd heard he had another job and spent some time at the Den, but didn't call it home. Everything beyond that was wild speculation. He'd either had a sub who'd shattered his soul or he was heartless to begin with and had never allowed anyone close.

All she knew was that she appreciated the way he ran the house. Nothing happened here without Gregorio or Master Damien knowing about it. Some of the playrooms had an exposed wall in case the players wanted to be seen. Other places had doors for privacy, but even then, there were windows so that someone could periodically check on the sub's safety.

To her knowledge, no one had ever witnessed Master Damien participating in a scene. Maggie knew she wasn't the only one who'd wanted to play with him.

"Is there a private room available?" David asked.

"First door on the right."

David wound up the leash again, bringing her in close. "I'd like you to keep your hands behind your back," he reminded her.

She immediately did as requested, but he continued to regard her. "Yes, Mr Tomlinson," she said. While she was accustomed to having Master Damien look in on her scenes, being corrected in front of him embarrassed her. She looked at the floor, wishing it would open up so she could disappear.

"Let me know if you need anything," Master Damien said.

"Thank you," David replied, answering for both of them.

She felt a tug on her leash. It had the effect of yanking her out of her musings and refocusing her on her submission. She forgot about herself and her feelings as she followed him down the hallway.

Once he had led her to the room and the reality of what they were about to do set in, the first tendrils of nerves rippled through her.

From her numerous visits, the room was familiar. Each of the play spaces had similarities — they were all stocked with cuffs and various spanking implements. But each room also catered to a different form of play. This one had a table that resembled something out of a doctor's office, but not exactly. There appeared to be a cradle for her head, so that she could safely be situated facedown. In that way, it looked more like something a massage therapist would use.

Like a table in a doctor's office, it had a small shelf that could be slid back, leaving her bottom hanging suspended. How much pressure she'd be under would depend entirely on how he secured her. There were attachments that could be extended for her heels. She had no idea how he intended to use the piece of furniture, but the numerous possibilities intrigued her as much as they made her anxious.

He closed the door behind them.

She knew the walls had been soundproofed. It could be disconcerting to others to overhear screaming, and when she was the one screaming, she liked having some privacy. Since the Den also served as a studio for exclusive video shoots, keeping down outside noise was important. Despite the extensive efforts, the walls still seemed to softly vibrate from Evan C's band.

David detached her leash. "Please kneel while I set up the room." He pointed to a spot on the floor.

The instruction at least was expected, something familiar in the oddness of sceneing with him.

He stood still while she lowered herself in position.

Maggie rarely played with the same man twice. There was something about the thrill of the unknown with a new Dom. The fact she knew David, but in a different context, enhanced her excitement and apprehension.

Since he hadn't instructed otherwise, she watched him hang the leash from a hook in the wall before placing his bag on the countertop. He unzipped it and pulled out several condoms—he hadn't been joking when he'd said he wanted to fuck her.

He laid out various sized cuffs, likely some for her wrists and others for her ankles. He pulled out a tawse, a paddle and three different floggers, each crafted from different coloured leather. The strands varied in thickness. Her mouth watered as she wondered which he'd select and if she'd ever get to try them all.

She knew him to be organised, and he never went home for the evening without putting away each pen, pencil and piece of paper. He arranged every item on the counter, with nothing touching. She hoped that precision extended to the way he would deal with her.

There were other items she couldn't see without craning her neck, and that would be bad form.

She did see him take out a bottle of water before he placed his bag on the floor and turned back to her.

Those dratted nerves returned, double time.

Without speaking, he picked up a chair and moved it close to where she knelt.

After sitting, he finally shattered the quiet by telling her, "Please stand and remove all your clothes." He offered his hand to help her up.

His grip was strong, firm, reassuring. Their bodies were close, and the setting pulsed with intimacy.

He released her, and she drew her shirt over her head.

"Purple?" he asked. "Another surprise. I'm betting the panties match the bra."

"Why would you guess that, Mr Tomlinson?"

"The bra isn't as risqué as I expected. Therefore I figured you bought a matched set."

He was right.

She dropped the shirt to the floor before unzipping the skirt and wriggling out of it. Maggie felt as if she were doing a striptease for him.

"Very nice," he said as he swept his gaze down her body, taking in her thong, stockings and garter belt.

Now she was doubly glad she'd made the purchases.

She stepped away from the skirt.

"Do you dress this way at work?"

"You'll never know, Mr Tomlinson."

The air seemed to hum with a sudden electrical current, like she'd felt in lightning storms on high mountain peaks. She hadn't meant it to sound like a challenge, but it had come out that way.

"Please continue," he said into the seething tension.

The first few minutes with a new Dom always made her uneasy, until she slid into the place where nothing interfered with her thought process, where doubts buckled beneath the heartbeat of instinct.

Aware of his scrutiny, she reached behind her and unhooked the bra clasp before drawing the straps down her arms. Still looking at him, she dropped the lacy lingerie and pulled her shoulders back.

He tapped his forefingers together. "You have gorgeous breasts," he said. "How sensitive are your nipples?"

"Not very," she replied. Beneath his scrutiny and the room's overhead fan, they began to bead. "When I masturbate, I need a lot of stimulation, so I put clamps on them."

"And would you like me to put a pair on you this evening?"

"If it pleases you, Sir. I mean, yes, please, Mr Tomlinson."

"I understand why you're the company's lead salesperson," he said with a slight nod of respect. "You're highly adaptable. This side of you that wants to please must be helpful in business development. It seems sincere."

"Thank you for saying so."

"You could try it when you enter my office."

"And you could release me from that employment contract."

"Without your talents, World Wide Now stands to lose a significant amount of sales revenue. If you opened a competing business or moved to one of our competitors, it could be up to forty per cent. So the answer is no."

The argument was a familiar one. If she were honest, she'd admit he was right. Their customers liked her. Her mother was the firm's creative talent, though. She had an eye for web branding, from actual design to implementation. Together they made a hell of a team, and customers were loyal to her mother, often returning for additional campaigns.

David stood and crossed to the counter. "Tweezers or clovers?"

"Clovers. That way you can tug on them and they'll stay in place," she said. "Please."

He selected a pair and tested the pressure on his little finger before discarding them in favour of a second set.

"Are those harder or lighter than the previous ones?" she asked.

"Harder."

Her pussy moistened. She waited with infinite patience for him to return.

"Offer your breasts to me."

For a moment, she looked at the clamps. A chain ran between them, and they hung from his index finger. Then she met his gaze, as if he'd urged her to look at him.

At work, he insisted on having his way. In this private room with just the two of them, her naked and vulnerable, him bare-chested and in charge, she saw him in a new way. There was a quiet, observant intensity in his blue eyes. He was listening to and respecting her every wish, changing his style to suit her while still asserting his will. That would make him an even better Dom. And she was looking forward to it.

Obediently she cupped her breasts, drawing them up and together. "Please, Mr Tomlinson, will you put the clamps on me?"

"It will be my pleasure."

The first touch of her boss's fingers on her skin sent shockwaves through her.

Before tonight, she would have said she'd never allow him to touch her. Now she was all but begging him to.

He played with her nipples, his touch extra light. She moaned, wanting more.

"I'll set the pace," he told her.

"Yes, Mr Tomlinson." Unable to help herself, she swayed towards him.

"So needy."

"Yes," she whispered.

He pinched her nipples then released the tips, only to grasp them again and roll the swollen peaks between his thumbs and forefingers.

"Oh, thank you. Thank you."

"Lovely manners you have, little one."

With her curves, she wasn't accustomed to being called little. Near him, she did feel small. He could tuck her under his chin and hold her close...not that she wanted him to, she told herself.

Most men gave her nipples a few perfunctory tugs, but he turned this torment into an art form.

He responded to her unspoken demand by increasing the pressure, making her nipples fully erect.

"Now they're ready. Keep holding your breasts," he instructed.

He let her go only long enough to take hold of her right nipple, extend it and affix the rubber tip.

"Ah!" She sucked in a breath.

"More than you thought?"

"Yes," she admitted.

"Can you bear it?"

The shock of it had already begun to fade as he took hold of her left nipple and stroked it, distracting her. "I'm fine, Mr Tomlinson," she said finally.

"You have expressive features. I'll have to watch you more carefully when we're together outside of here."

"I'm better at hiding my thoughts when I'm not aroused sexually," she told him. Before she was mentally prepared, he attached the second clamp, compressing her nipple.

She closed her eyes.

"At some point, I may add weights to them," he told her when she had centred herself and looked at him again.

"If it pleases you," she said.

"I'll give you a few more moments to adjust before I amuse myself with your tits." He took his seat again. "When you're ready, remove the rest of your clothes."

She worked down the ankle straps of her platform shoes then kicked them aside. The movement caused the clamps to sway, so she moved a bit slower.

"Beautiful," he approved. "Nothing pleases me more than this."

"Mr Tomlinson?"

"Your femininity. Your graceful motions."

Under his scrutiny, she removed the panties. She stood before him in nothing but the garter belt and black stockings.

"Nicely groomed," he said.

From his tone, she couldn't tell whether he approved of her shaving or not. She settled for saying, "Yes."

"I like my subs completely naked so I can see every red mark. Remove the rest of your lingerie if you please, Ms Carpenter, so we can get on with it."

She released each clasp and rolled down her stockings, one at a time, again taking care to minimise extra movements. Then she unfastened the hook behind her waist. She allowed the last of her garments to pool on the floor.

Under the scrutiny of his intense gaze, she fought the onslaught of nerves that urged her to cover herself.

"Very pretty," he said.

His tone sounded so sincere she believed him. Either that, or he was a skilled Dominant who knew how to put a sub at ease. It didn't matter. She gained confidence from his compliment.

"Turn all the way around. Slowly."

When she faced him again, he nodded in apparent satisfaction.

"As I've been fantasising about it, we're going to start with an old-fashioned over-the-knee spanking. But first..."

He stood again and retrieved some substantial-looking weights.

She reminded herself she'd given tacit agreement, but that didn't stop her from swallowing deeply as he approached her.

"I don't mind tears," he reminded her.

"Do you have onions in your pockets, Mr Tomlinson? That's the only way you'll see me cry."

"Defiant until the end, are you?"

Instead of immediately attaching them, he squeezed her breasts. Heat shot through her.

"I'm going to stroke your pussy."

Since he hadn't instructed her to part her legs or move, she stayed where she was. He plumped one of her breasts while he slid a finger between her labia. She felt herself becoming slicker as he masterfully coaxed a response from her.

"Could you come from just this?"

"I... I imagine I could, Mr Tomlinson." She wondered if he'd experiment, but he stopped and lowered his hand.

"I want you more aroused when I let you come."

"Of course, Sir." She'd been with enough Doms to know that some preferred she wait. Others enjoyed making her come multiple times. In case the evening didn't go as well as she hoped, she'd packed her trusty vibrator in her overnight bag.

"Ready for the weights?"

"Yes, Mr Tomlinson."

He grinned at her. "I do like the way that sounds."

"Don't get accustomed to it past this evening. At work I'm going to start calling you David."

"Cheekiness earns you extra spankings."

"I'm not afraid."

His smile faded, and once again he was all stern and fierce. Part of her knew she shouldn't torment him, that it was akin to pulling a tiger's tail, but this side of her boss intrigued her. At work, she didn't dare answer back. Her mother's future hung in the balance. But here... There was a certain freedom in being on footing that they both understood, that had rules. If things felt out of control, she could use her safe word. The truth was, for her, the dynamic they had elsewhere enhanced the scene, adding an air of danger.

Dispassionately, he added the weights. She did a little dance as her nipples were dragged downwards.

"Damn, that's beautiful," he said.

"It hurts."

"When you're a bit more aroused, you'll forget about it," he promised.

Though she knew he was right and she often moved from one set to another at home, having him in charge seemed to magnify the experience. She closed her eyes and gritted her teeth.

"Would you like to use your slow word in order to have me remove them?"

Maggie considered his question. She liked being pushed past what she thought she could endure. The pressure was tolerable, and she suspected it would enhance her spanking. And she knew it was one more experience she could relive while she masturbated during the coming weeks. Some things that she had disliked at the time added memorable detail to her fantasies. "Thank you for asking, Mr Tomlinson. I'm fine."

He fisted the chain and drew her onto her toes. She gasped for air, but damn, it turned her on as well.

"You're a perfect princess," he told her.

She closed her eyes, willing herself to surrender rather than struggle against the pain.

Suddenly he released his grip, but he captured her shoulders to steady her as she balanced again on her bare feet.

When she looked at him, she saw his gaze was intent, focused on her face. He had apparently been honest earlier when he'd said he would watch and enjoy her suffering.

Of all the Doms on the planet, she would never have expected to want to please him. But the look of approval in his deep, thoughtful eyes sent a shiver of submissive recognition through her.

"Now for that spanking."

He took her wrist and drew her with him to the chair. He sat. Her mouth dried. She could ask for a drink of water, but she knew it wouldn't help. She was parched from the sudden onslaught of trepidation, nothing more. For a moment, just a moment, she wondered if she'd been smart to goad him earlier. Now she was having second thoughts about exposing her buttocks to a man who obviously relished the idea of reddening her skin.

Suddenly this seemed all too real. It was more complex than her usual scene where she would say, 'I've been bad, Sir, please punish me'. Rather, this had the knife-edge of reality added to it.

Releasing her, he said, "Over my knee, Maggie."

She moved towards him. He offered a hand for support, but he didn't grip her. Symbolically he was letting her know it was her choice.

He helped her into position.

The weights on her clamps pulled her breasts and nipples towards the floor — the pain was relentless.

Beneath her belly, his thighs felt strong. He was an unyielding Dom. The denim was rough against her skin, and the coolness from his handcuffs teased her hip for a fraction of a second.

He jostled her so she was more secure. He placed his large palm in the middle of her back.

She expected him to trap her legs between his, but he didn't.

"I want to see you flail. If you try to get away, I want to drag you back. A little resistance from the fairer sex does me good."

He traced a finger up the inside of her right thigh, making her tremble. He flitted across her pussy, sliding just a fingertip inside her.

"Such a responsive princess."

He rubbed her thighs and buttocks with light motions. As he continued, he used a bit more force.

She tried to relax, but anxiety held her motionless.

He didn't ask if she was ready, instead he swatted her hard. She cried out from the impact and she squirmed, making the clamps jump. *"Damn."*

"We haven't even started."

It certainly felt like it to her.

He smacked her again, burning her buttocks.

"Your skin turns pink quickly. Do you bruise?"

Without waiting for an answer, he seared her skin again, this time on her right thigh.

Though she had intended to remain still and calmly take anything he gave, she flailed about. Each motion jerked her breasts, increasing the agony in her nipples.

He shocked her by moving her onto her side so that she was facing him. The position changed the angle of his impact.

For self-preservation, she curled against him. The dichotomy awed her — she was seeking stability from his body while he mercilessly beat her.

"Your ass was made for this," he told her.

He rained painful spanks across her rear. She drank in great gulps of air, trying to reach a peaceful space deep inside her head. Normally when she received this kind of physical stimulation, she was able to exult in it. David — the Dom — didn't afford her that luxury. His smacks were random, some horrible, others almost gentle. He didn't pause between them. Instead he blazed them everywhere, keeping her on edge. Her brain couldn't process the information fast enough to figure out where he was going to strike next. She was wading in darkened waters, yet she didn't want to end it.

He spanked the tender flesh below her buttocks. The force jolted her. The weights jangled together and she was assaulted by gripping pain. As a way to centre herself, she tried to count the hits, but she was unable to. This man brought determination to everything he did.

Almost without her noticing, he slowed down the number of spanks.

Warmth bathed her body.

David sat her up and drew her against his chest. Her limbs felt numb, so when he placed her head against his shoulder, she didn't protest.

He stroked her hair and said words that sounded nonsensical.

She heard the steady thud of his heart, and it gave her comfort.

"I'm going to take off the clamps," he told her. "Hopefully your nipples are sore enough that my touching them later will hurt."

He cupped her right breast tightly and parted the rubber-tipped clamp. He pinched her nipple and squeezed it several times, allowing circulation to return by measures.

"Ah... Thank you, Mr Tomlinson." Often her Doms released the clamps and allowed blood to rush back in painfully.

He repeated the process with the other side.

By the time he finished, she was holding herself away from him a bit.

"How was your spanking?"

She gazed into his eyes. This was somehow more intimate than having her pussy exposed to him. She inhaled his scent.

His chest was more than broad, it was inviting. The HM band emphasised the ripple of his biceps. If she were the type of woman to lean on a man, she'd be tempted to rest against him again.

As he had earlier, he pushed hair back from her face. His eyebrows were furrowed. She fought an insane urge to smooth his forehead. Instead she clasped her hands together. "Fine, Mr Tomlinson," she said.

"Fine?"

Remembering he'd mentioned protocols earlier, she added, "Thank you for your attention."

"You wouldn't be punished for that omission since I hadn't instructed you beforehand. Rules must be understood ahead of time. Still, good manners are always appropriate behaviour. Continue about the spanking."

"I haven't experienced anything quite like it."

"In what way?"

"I've never had a punishment, only a scene."

"I told you I've imagined having you over my knee. And it wasn't erotic and meant to get you off, but it was far from punitive."

"Mr Tomlinson?"

"We don't have a permanent relationship. Therefore, I am not in the position to mete our actual punishment. This spanking wasn't delivered with the idea of correcting persistent or offensive behaviour. Well, maybe the offensive behaviour." His quick smile took any sting from his words. "If I had punished you, you would have known it. There would have been no pleasure in it at all."

"So…"

"It was more of a test, than anything."

She frowned.

"I wanted to gauge your reactions, see what you disliked, what you liked, notice how your skin responded, where you're most sensitive, what made you wince or cry out or sigh." He threaded his fingers into her hair and pulled back her head.

"Did I pass the test?" she asked.

"Princess, you could not have failed."

Again, words that took her off guard. Was he simply a very considerate Dom? Or a man deeper than she'd believed possible from what she knew about him?

Another thought followed that. He'd said he was learning about her, but she'd discovered a number of things about him, too. He paid attention to her. He hadn't taken her too far, and he had given her enough that she wasn't rolling her eyes or pretending it was hard enough so that she didn't damage his fragile ego.

"And when you're ready, I want to tie you to the table and torment you."

"Is there an orgasm involved in that?"

"I wouldn't dream of sending you home unsatisfied."

"How about two?" she asked. "Or am I pushing it, Mr Tomlinson?"

"Greedy sub."

"I prefer the word needy," she corrected.

He inclined his head towards the apparatus that came complete with extensions for her limbs. "Shall we find out just how needy?"

Restlessness filled her. The spanking had left her wanting more, emotionally as well as physically. "Yes, please."

He tugged her hair a little harder. "In that case, lie on your back with your head in the cradle." Without another word, he slid her from his lap.

Chapter Three

Damn. This woman, this sub, delighted him.

David watched Maggie's every move, much as he had for the last few months. Ever since he'd first been introduced to her, he'd been partial to her curves and the elegant way she carried herself. The pencil skirts she favoured during business hours were professional, but the way they hugged her full ass inspired some thoughts that were not appropriate in a work environment.

At the office, she kept her black hair pulled back, wore minimal makeup and her shirts were never revealing.

When he'd seen her there tonight, sipping her drink, her hair spilling invitingly over her shoulders, dressed in a short skirt, tight top, platform shoes instead of pumps and topped off with a sparkly collar, he'd looked twice. At first glance, he hadn't been able to believe she was the same woman who challenged him on a daily basis. She'd looked soft and approachable, so different from the woman who'd once entered his office without knocking, slamming the door behind her, making the solid wood jump in its casing.

She'd stalked over on her sensible, I-mean-business-and-won't-be-intimidated-by-you pumps, had planted her hands on top of his polished desk then leaned towards him and threatened to quit if he downsized and released a certain employee.

For five minutes, she'd presented a logical—if heated—case for keeping the overhead so high.

Her passion had captivated him. Her employment contract was ironclad. Her mother would lose out on a significant amount of money if Maggie walked away. That meant she had a lot to lose. So if she were willing to put that on the line for a co-worker, he'd listen.

She'd convinced him. To her credit, she had not gloated.

From that confrontation, amongst others, he'd taken her for a strait-laced, if not uptight, woman who might be sexually repressed. That hadn't stopped him from imagining her luscious ass upturned over his lap as he spanked her. On many occasions, he'd jacked off in the shower with that picture in his mind, particularly after she had annoyed the hell out of him at work.

Reality surpassed fantasy.

Maggie Carpenter was as intriguing as she was responsive. She had told him earlier that she would encourage him to move faster, but he doubted she would need to. When he'd hit her hard, she'd made mewing sounds and had kicked her legs. It seemed he hadn't got her close to tears, but the blows had definitely been hard enough to secure her attention.

After keeping her waiting in silence for two full minutes, he stood. The chair legs scraped the floor. She didn't try to see what he was doing, but he saw her belly move as she took a breath. "No doubt you've had some formal training," he said as he walked around her.

She followed him with her gaze. "I've had a little bit, Mr Tomlinson. I took some classes at a club in Denver. And I've had relationships that had a few BDSM elements."

He was discovering more and more layers to Maggie. Their remaining time together wouldn't be nearly enough to uncover them all. "Extend your arms."

Unhesitatingly, she did so. He adjusted the table so that her arms were at a gentle stretch, nothing terribly uncomfortable, but not too much give, either. She'd be helpless in her bondage.

"Now your legs," he told her. He tied her ankles then strapped down her thighs. Next, he moved apart the table's legs, so that her pussy was wide open and available. "Too bad I can't keep you like this at the office."

"In your dreams, Mr Tomlinson."

"Yours as well, Ms Carpenter."

She shivered a little. Oh, yes. Doubtless his defiant employee would remember this. Perhaps she'd walk into his office on Monday morning and picture herself over his desk. Or maybe battle a compulsion to strip and kneel for him? It was impossible, he knew, but he couldn't banish the thought. "Are you comfortable enough?"

"It's a bit of a stretch, but nothing that is causing muscle cramps."

"You can squirm without injuring anything?"

"It shouldn't be a problem."

"Shall we find out?" He touched her clit.

She tightened her buttocks and pulled back a little.

"How was that? And I'm not talking about your cunt. I'm asking if you experienced any discomfort in your thighs or arms."

"I'm fine, Sir."

He was going to enjoy this experience immensely. Bringing off the woman who constantly confronted him would be a great pleasure, better, he imagined, than spanking her had been. Listening to her cries as she called his name and begged for his touch would be intoxicating. "I'm planning to flog you, Maggie," he said.

"Thank you, Mr Tomlinson."

His cock hardened. He was trying to give her a way out in case she didn't want a dozen strands of leather biting at her flesh, especially since she was face up, leaving her most tender flesh exposed. Instead, she encouraged him.

He walked to the counter and selected a flogger with fairly thick strands before returning to her. Her nipples were pebbled, and he could still see small indentations from the bite of the clamps. "So inviting," he said.

"Please."

He'd never been with a woman who seemed to enjoy nipple play as much as she did. He laid the flogger across her body, just above her pubic bone.

David pinched the pretty pink tips gently, watching her reactions.

She sighed.

He did it again and she closed her eyes.

The third time, he held on tight and pulled hard, distending her nipples and forcing her to arch her back and shift in her restraints.

Her abandon was intoxicating.

David released her only to take hold again, squeezing brutally, rolling the flesh for added pain.

This time, she breathed hard and opened her eyes, fixing her gaze on his. Trust was reflected in the wide, liquid, brown depths.

He continued to watch her reactions as he pulled up even farther. Her breaths were forced out in little bursts, but she never protested.

She didn't gasp until he released her. "Sexy, Maggie." He stroked her pussy, not surprised to find her moist. Damn, he wanted to take her hard, now. But he'd promised her an orgasm or two, and he intended to deliver.

Telling himself the wait would make it better for him, he moved between her legs, leaving the flogger where it was. "I'm going to move back the part of the table where your butt is resting."

She moved, ineffectually—his restraints prevented her from moving more than a fraction of an inch.

Within moments, her bottom had nothing beneath it. Even if she wanted to, she couldn't escape his lash. "Your damp cunt is a beautiful sight, Maggie."

David moved away to take off his clothes then picked up the flogger. "I want you to cry."

"I won't."

"There's not a part of you from the chest down that will escape me," he told her. The ability to mark all her skin was one of the reasons he favoured a flogger. He didn't have to be as cautious as he was when utilising a crop or cane. He just needed to be careful about the distance and power he used.

He started with the soles of her feet, using the leather lightly. She groaned just a little.

"Ticklish?"

"Not particularly, Mr Tomlinson. That's just..."

He waited.

"New."

"And…"

"Ah!"

He studied her reactions. That wasn't pain on her face, more like confusion.

Before she could become too accustomed, he moved to the front of her feet, including her toes before working on her ankles. He loved to mix things up for his subs, giving them a wide variety of sensations. He didn't mind staying in one place if he was giving an orgasm, but otherwise, he wanted her entire body sensitised.

He continued with her calves, knees and the fronts of her thighs, flicking his wrist and alternating on each of her legs. He skipped over her pussy and went straight for her stomach.

"Mr Tomlinson," she protested.

"In due time," he promised.

"Fuck," she said.

As much as possible, since there was no support for her bottom and she was partially suspended, she tilted her pelvis, as if that would change his mind.

"You're submitting to my pleasure," he reminded her.

"I thought we were getting to an orgasm."

"You're not nearly ready enough," he said.

She gritted her teeth.

"You're adorable when you're mad," he said.

"I am not adorable," she insisted.

He lashed her belly.

She cried out. But at least he'd silenced her argument.

"You've got a perfect body," he told her. He loved her softness. He knew she watched her weight, and he'd seen her refuse the pastries that people brought into the office. From what he'd observed, she allowed herself the luxury of an unpronounceable frothy coffee drink only on Fridays. "Made for beatings and sex," he added.

"I—"

"That's my opinion and, at the moment, the only one that matters. Say, 'Yes, Mr Tomlinson'."

She pursed her lips.

He withheld the lash. "Say it."

Her exhalation was anything but agreeable or feminine. "Yes, Mr Tomlinson."

He immediately resumed his attention.

She relaxed her body again, an outward sign of her submission in a way that was considerably more meaningful than any mere words would ever be.

In submission, he'd learnt actions should be more carefully regarded than what was said. People lied all the time, small untruths mainly, as they tried to spare others from hurt or hide their own feelings. In that regard, he supposed, a scene wasn't much different from any other area of life. Employees and associates, even professionals he hired, often told him what they thought he wanted to hear. But gestures revealed what lay beneath the veneer.

When she either accepted defeat or claimed victory, her entire being lost its tension.

Keeping her off guard, he switched up his pattern. After whipping her ribs, he flogged her arms and shoulders.

"Sir is driving me mad," she said, her voice a whisper.

"Is that right?" he asked unconcernedly. At his own pace, he moved over her collarbone then down her chest.

"I want…"

"Tell me," he said. He knew what she was going to say, it was obvious, but still, he liked to hear the words.

"Attention."

"I'll make sure I give you everything you can take," he promised.

"On my breasts, Mr Tomlinson. And my pussy. I'm getting horny."

He wished he hadn't asked. Pre-cum leaked from his cockhead. He wanted to give her everything she desired and it took considerable focus to continue on his planned path. The longer he took, the more aroused she would be.

Finally he reached her breasts. He wanted to leave marks that she would see when she dressed for work on Monday.

Her nipples were still hard. He caught the tips and areolas with the very edge of the leather, flicking his wrist quickly to brutally bite at the flesh.

She screamed over and over, thrashing her head.

"Good," he said. "Very good. Give me all of your emotions." He adjusted the grip on the handle of the flogger so he could hit her with the broad sides of the leather strands rather than with the tips.

She cried out when he caught the underside of her creamy flesh, but she continued to arch towards him rather than trying to escape.

David took great care with her, ensuring all pain was deliberately inflicted.

She rewarded his efforts with tiny moans punctuated with screams.

Without warning her, he let the strands fall on her pussy.

"Yes. *Damn.* Yes."

He blazed across her inner thighs and her pussy, giving her no quarter as each piece of leather fell, bit, caressed. He liked the way her most private part was exposed with no way for her to pull away even when he stopped holding back.

Within a minute or two, her breathing settled into a regular pattern. Everything he dished up, she hungrily accepted. "Pain slut," he said.

"More, more, more," she chanted.

Her wild abandon had earned her an orgasm.

He rubbed the flogger's handle between her slick folds as he swiftly entered her pussy with two fingers.

"I want to come," she said.

"Beg." He decreased the pressure, giving her just enough to keep her on edge but not enough to kick her over it.

"Oh, God, please. Please, Mr Tomlinson, for all that is holy, let me fucking come."

"That's not exactly what I had in mind, Ms Carpenter."

She struggled for purchase. After gasping a couple of times, she said, "Please, Mr Tomlinson, I'm begging you. Please let me come."

Much better. He finger-fucked her hard as he stimulated her clitoris.

"Sir? Please. Mr Tomlinson."

He saw her whole body shake as she fought to obey him and suppress the imminent orgasm. He'd known her for months, and he wondered if he'd been blind. She was perfect in her responses. "Come," he instructed. "Come *now*."

Maggie moved against him faster and faster, and he responded to her silent demands, pushing harder, finding her G-spot and pressing against it.

Her body became racked with tremors and she screamed out her orgasm.

He continued his motions until she shivered a bit. He eased the handle away from her and slowly withdrew from her heated cunt.

She blew out a breath and pulled against the restraints.

"You're a very sexy woman, Maggie." He walked around to the top of the table, keeping a hand on her at all times in reassurance. Her body was pink, with several deep red patches. He turned her head so that she faced him as he stood next to her. "That was one," he said. "Think you're up for more?"

"Are you challenging me now, Mr Tomlinson?" she asked quietly.

"Not at all."

She raised a sceptical eyebrow.

"Okay," he admitted. "Perhaps."

"Give me your best, Mr Tomlinson. I can take it."

He grinned. This was the Maggie he knew, the Maggie he respected and admired. She was so unlike any sub he'd been involved with. Of course he knew tough-minded businesswomen, a few athletes, even a politician. Yet Maggie's exterior, combined with her complex and demanding vulnerability, ensnared him. "I'd like to leave you restrained."

"If it pleases you, Mr Tomlinson."

"I need to know if your body is able to tolerate the stress."

"I'm not uncomfortable."

"In that case..." Satisfied she was all right mentally as well as physically, he donned a condom and fetched the clamps again.

Her eyes had widened and she tracked his every move.

He removed the weights before saying, "You've had enough of a break, I think."

"I'm sure you know best, Mr Tomlinson."

"How is it that no one has beaten you for your impudent tone?"

She gave an impish smile. "There's been no need as I'm always sincere."

"Honest, too."

"You have a beautiful cock, Mr Tomlinson."

Her statement caught him off guard.

"I hadn't really noticed you were naked until now," she added.

Her scrutiny made him harder.

"Are you going to fuck me with it? Surely you're not going to let that erection go to waste?"

"Sub—"

"I could suck it for you, Sir."

"That's one way to shut you up."

"It's effective, too," she agreed.

The mechanics of that were difficult, but not impossible. He held her head in one palm and brought her closer to him. It stretched her neck, but she didn't protest. Instead, she stuck out her tongue, seeking his cock. With his free hand, he stroked his shaft. Then he guided it towards her mouth.

She pressed her tongue against the underneath of his cock and opened wide to accept him. He noticed she'd closed her eyes and was making little sounds of pleasure. He'd had his dick sucked dozens, maybe hundreds of times, and he enjoyed it more when he knew his sub was into it.

She took him as deep as she could with the awkward position, and she strained against her cuffs, trying to use her hands. The image combined with the sensation of her tongue and suction of her mouth was almost enough to make him spill.

When she slid up, he squeezed her jaw and withdrew his cock. "Not so fast."

"But, Mr Tomlinson, I was enjoying that, and I want—"

"Quiet," he instructed. "This is about what I want."

She looked at him, but she closed her mouth.

"Smart princess," he said.

Maggie snapped her teeth together.

"That was a little disrespectful," he warned her.

"Of course you're right, Mr Tomlinson. I'm sorry."

Though she might have used the right words, she'd chosen the wrong tone. And she glared at him rather than looking away to express her contrition. And with the basic training she'd had, no doubt she knew the difference.

He crouched next to her, dug a hand into her hair and yanked her head back.

Her eyes widened from the pain.

"If you have something you want to discuss, say so. But I won't tolerate that type of behaviour either here or outside the Den." He chose his next words deliberately to emphasise the differences in their stations as well as his displeasure. "Am I clear, sub?"

"Crystal, Mr Tomlinson."

He loosened his grip on her hair.

"I object to you being condescending with the princess comment."

"Thank you for saying what's on your mind." He traced the pad of his thumb across her cheekbone. Keeping his voice soft and gentle, he said, "I was not being condescending, Maggie. It was simply an acknowledgement that I recognised your compliance and that you'd chosen the correct path. I liked the way you were sucking my dick, and I appreciate that you would have continued. But I have a scene in mind and that was not part of it. I should hope you know me well enough to know I respect you and your brain. Here, I need you to trust me."

She blinked. "I..."

"Communicate with me, Maggie, all times, about all things. I will forgive your mockery this once, but with the warning that next time, retribution will be swift."

She shuddered.

"Any further questions?"

"No, Sir, Mr Tomlinson."

"Then tell me you understand what I said."

"I should communicate with you. Sarcasm has no place between us, and you will punish me if I use it again."

"Perfect," he said. "You agree to that stipulation?"

"I do, Sir."

"Then we're clear."

"I'm sorry," she whispered.

Her sincerity undid him. "I accept your apology," he said. By slow measures, he released his tight grip on her hair. He also dropped his other hand so that he wasn't touching her and influencing her decision when he asked, "Shall we continue?"

She bit into her lower lip, appearing thoughtful.

A few seconds passed without her responding. Finally she spoke. "I'd like to."

David debated his next action, aware of his responsibilities to her, to them, to the scene. Tension lingered in the atmosphere, and he knew she needed to feel forgiven and emotionally safe. "Do you need me to loosen or remove any of your cuffs?"

"No, Mr Tomlinson."

As he stood, he placed a kiss on her forehead.

She inhaled and held the breath.

"How do you feel about butt plugs?"

She was forced to exhale so she could answer. "Sir?"

He kept a careful eye on her as he crossed to the counter. Seeing he had her attention, he held up a rather large glass plug.

"Yikes," she said.

He had no intention of starting her with that one, but she didn't need to know that. She just needed to slip back into the correct state of mind before he touched her sexually again. "Do you object to me using it on you?"

"I am okay with anal, Mr Tomlinson. That just seems a bit extreme."

"And if it's my pleasure?"

For a moment, she was silent. When she spoke, her voice was soft and a bit uncertain. "Then I will do whatever you ask."

He believed her. Since she said she had some experience, he settled on one that was medium sized. Made from surgical grade stainless steel, this was one of his favourites—it had a circle on the end that he could place his finger through and move it as he desired.

"I'll make sure you're prepared first."

"Sir is too kind."

"I presume you'll be appreciative?"

"Most certainly, Mr Tomlinson."

After coating his forefinger with lubricant, he returned to her. He pressed his finger against her tightest hole. "Open up," he told her while easing in as far as his first knuckle. He withdrew then re-entered, stretching her as he went. "Relax, pet."

He knew that wasn't necessarily easy as there was no support beneath her hips. But it also prevented her from pulling away.

After several strokes, he sank his finger all the way inside and wiggled it about a bit to stretch her.

She exhaled softly. "Mmm," she said.

"That sounds like pleasure."

"It is. I'm ready for more if it suits you, Mr Tomlinson."

"You are into this." She had warned him that she would ask for more rather than using a safe word.

"I don't get to scene as often as I would like, so I want to enjoy every moment."

"Anything to ensure your satisfaction," he told her. He crossed to the counter, rinsed his hands then rolled on a condom before liberally dousing the plug with lube.

In the few seconds he was gone, he heard her slight movements as she adjusted her body against her restraints. She seemed somewhat restless with his absence. He wasn't sure why that delighted him so much, but it did. Perhaps it was because of her independent, self-confident air. Regardless, she silently communicated her need of his dominance, and every male instinct responded.

She stiffened when he placed the tip at the entrance to her anus.

"That's cold," she protested.

"Shall I warm it for you next time, princess?"

"Whatever you desire, Sir," she responded.

"Don't think I'm not storing up a list of your cheeky transgressions. A little gratitude that I didn't put it on ice wouldn't be amiss."

"You'd do that?"

"Try me."

"This feels just fine," she said hurriedly. "Thank you for your kindness and generosity, Mr Tomlinson."

As she'd spoken, he'd worked the metal inside her, twisting it slightly as he pushed before pulling it back. He used restrained motions, giving her only a little at a time. Her words had been partially bravado, if the way she tightened the muscles in her legs was any indication. The plug had a considerably larger girth than his finger. "You're almost there," he assured her as he neared the biggest part.

He ached to have his cock in her. With the angle of her pelvis and the fact her back channel would be stuffed, the tight fit would be orgasm inducing.

She whimpered.

"It's almost in." He gave a firm push, and once the fattest part was past her sphincter, the rest slid in, the base resting against her.

She sighed and shifted as she accommodated the intrusion and its not-insignificant weight. He gave a quick twist with the hook.

"I... That's..."

"It's in, and I think I inserted it rather nicely, instead of with a single shove."

"Thank you, Mr Tomlinson."

"I like it much better when you use your manners," he said approvingly. He stepped back to look at her. The silver protruded, refracting light. Her eyes were closed. Thick, dark hair spilled everywhere in untamed, pretty disarray. Her nipples were still hard, and goosebumps dotted her lower arms.

Her body was spread wide for him, as if in invitation.

"Please do me," she whispered, straining to lift her head so she could look at him.

"Perfect princess," he responded. He squatted between her legs and parted her labia to lick her pussy.

She struggled against the restraints, seeking purchase with her heels.

"Mr Tomlinson! Sir!"

Instead of giving her permission to orgasm, he teased her clit with his tongue. He moved the plug inside her, rotating it as he gently tugged then eased it back in.

She cried out.

Her responses were pure, making his cock even harder, something that generally didn't happen unless he stroked himself.

"I want you in me," she said around a gasp.

He continued to torment her until she jerked against his mouth in unspoken demand. Then he stopped.

She slowly relaxed her body, but didn't protest his denial. Instead, she said, "Thank you for your attention."

His sub certainly knew how to behave. "I'll make sure you're rewarded for your behaviour."

"The only thing I want is your pleasure, Mr Tomlinson," she said.

"Clever pet." He stood, taking care to keep a reassuring hand on her. He placed his cockhead at her pussy's entrance. In silent entreaty, she moved towards him as much as her bonds would allow. Damn, this woman knew how to hit all his sexual hot buttons.

He took his cock in hand and began to enter her.

She blew air out through her pursed lips. "That's tight... Oh."

"Damn." With the plug as big as it was, he didn't have a lot of space. "Tell me if I need to stop."

"It's… Don't stop. Just…overwhelming."

He nodded. "I don't want to hurt you."

"I want to feel everything," she replied.

Restraining his urges was more difficult than he might have imagined. The time playing with her, rough as well as gentle, had banked his desires. He wanted to slam into her, fuck her, ride her, claim her, let her know that — right now — she belonged to him.

"Take me."

"Patience, princess." He put his thumb against her clit and manipulated the sensitive flesh.

"Sir! Oh, Mr Tomlinson, I need to come."

"While I'm fucking you, you can come as often as you like." Concentrating solely on her satisfaction took all of his self-control. He kept his thrusts shallow and continued to toy with her, peeling back the hood of her clit so that he had greater access to that bundle of nerves.

She tightened her buttocks.

"Sir!"

He stroked her faster.

"Please, please put your cock all the way in me."

Even if he'd wanted to, he could deny her nothing. He buried himself so deep his testicles touched the hook on the end of her plug.

"Fuck me, Mr Tomlinson."

He rocked inside her with short, shallow motions.

She screamed as she came. Her pussy muscles contracted around him, almost driving his orgasm, but David forced himself to hold off. He wanted her to shatter at least one more time.

When her body stilled, she whispered, "That was okay."

"Princess, you're a glutton for punishment."

She smiled a little to show she'd been teasing and that she was drained.

It had been a long time since he'd enjoyed fucking a woman as much.

"The plug intensifies everything," she said. "Well, along with Sir's massive cock."

He withdrew enough to lightly slap her cunt. "Of course."

"Keep that up, Mr Tomlinson and I'll be coming again."

"That's the intention."

She squeezed her eyes shut. "I'm not sure I'll survive the night."

"Good."

Once her breathing had evened out, he began to thrust again, this time, in long, slow movements.

"Oh," she murmured.

He changed his angle so that he could grasp her nipples and pull up hard, adding a small amount of pain to the mix.

"Damn," she said, fighting against her bonds.

If she were free, he knew she'd wrap her legs around his waist, but he liked having her like this, at his mercy, even if the other way appealed. "Come for me," he told her, twisting her swollen flesh.

She tossed her head as she whimpered then forced her shoulders down against the padding.

So, so fucking sexy.

Her insides tightened and she milked his cock. He could no longer hold back. He jerked his hips, feeling the rigidity of the stainless steel that filled her ass, a sensation-filled contrast with the soft wetness of her cunt.

"Do it," she begged. "Do *me*."

Her reactions to the erotic beating and to the sex were open. It was obvious that, to her, this was no act. The purity of her response was what he hoped to find every time he scened with a woman. Ever since he'd been introduced to BDSM in his early twenties, he hadn't been interested in vanilla sex. Giving a woman more than she knew was possible appealed to him. This experience with Maggie, though, went beyond that. Satisfying her was of utmost importance to him. The way she embraced everything he offered, enhanced his enjoyment.

He released her nipples and grabbed her hips, tilting them and holding her in place.

Lost in her surrender, David fucked her hard. The bass from the music outside drove him. He had to have this woman. Now.

He froze. A fraction of a second later, hot cum spurted, filling the condom. He stood there, saying nothing, holding her, his cock still thick.

A last bit surged up, making him feel drained.

"Yum," she said. "Thank you."

He released his grip on her hips.

"I hope I get bruises there," she said.

David gave a wry smile. "That wasn't my intention, princess. I generally have more control during an orgasm."

"The way you made me come... I'm glad you had the same reaction," she whispered.

When he'd invited her to play, he hadn't thought much beyond spanking her ass. He hadn't anticipated that the woman who fought him so much would be so captivating, that he'd want to know her more.

He withdrew from her.

After disposing of the condom, he crossed the room to give her bottom some support and release her arms.

"Take your time," he cautioned, rubbing her shoulders and wrists.

"Ow," she said.

"Take your time," he repeated. "When you're ready, I'm going to remove the butt plug."

"I, ah, I can do that myself, Mr Tomlinson."

"Embarrassment at this point, Maggie?"

"That seems a little personal," she admitted.

"Get over it."

She turned her head to one side.

He teased her pussy to focus her attention while he pulled out the plug. "Not so bad, was it?"

"If you say so."

"It's not too late to give you a few more swats."

"I was agreeing with you, Sir."

"Ah." He went to the sink and washed the plug and his hands before loosening the bonds securing her legs. He massaged her lower legs, then worked the area of her hip flexors.

"Do I have to tip you, Mr Tomlinson?" she asked when he was done.

"I consider this part of the service," he replied, helping her to sit. "How does your body feel?"

She wiggled her toes and fingers. "Well used." She smiled. "Thank you, Sir."

He offered a hand to steady her as she eased from the table.

While he pulled on his jeans, she slid back into her stockings, moving her body in an appealing, feminine way. "This is almost as erotic as seeing you naked," he said. He folded his arms across his chest and watched her clip the garter belt to the stockings, all the while wondering if he could revise the company dress code to require she wear this to work every day.

Immediately he nixed that idea.

He'd get nothing done.

She stepped into the skirt. All the time, she'd avoided putting on the bra. He wondered if it was intentional.

Finally she did put on the purple lingerie, and he was pretty damn sure he'd spend a lot of time in the future fantasising about taking it back off her.

She fought with the tight shirt, so he stepped in. "Sorry, I can't stand there and watch you struggle," he said, taking the material from her.

Though her eyes widened, she didn't protest.

He helped her into the shirt and smoothed it into place.

She kept her fingertips on his forearm as she slipped into her shoes.

"Make me a promise, Mr Tomlinson?"

He inclined his head.

"Don't wear that armband to work."

"Too much of a reminder about who you really are and where you belong?"

She betrayed her inner thoughts by looking at the floor before unblinkingly meeting his gaze. "The HM stands for House Monitor, not His Majesty," she said saucily. "I want you to remember that."

David extrapolated from her statement. "No authority over you outside of the Den?"

"None."

He traced her collar. "Then don't wear this again until you're ready to cede authority for your sexual satisfaction to me."

Her sweet, sexy lips parted. Then she blinked, breaking the momentary spell she'd held him under. "Enjoy the rest of your evening, Mr Tomlinson."

"Likewise, Ms Carpenter."

Without another word, she turned and exited the room before closing the door with a decisive *snick*.

It bothered him that she'd vanished before he could ensure she was completely okay. He'd hoped to spend a few minutes caring for her, even talking. He wished she'd waited long enough to at least have a few sips of water.

Christ. She might not have needed a few minutes of aftercare, but he needed to give them.

In the past, he'd been accused of being relentless. He didn't take time off for vacations, and had caused trouble on his honeymoon when his bride had caught him on his laptop in the middle of the night. During stressful times, he'd get in two workouts. He didn't require much sleep and he had boundless energy. He saw each day as a task list and he methodically checked things off and kept moving.

Until Maggie, he'd had no urge to soothe a woman he'd beaten. Lack of cuddling and intimacy had decimated his marriage.

By the time he'd pulled his boots back on, washed his toys, packed his bag, collected the leash and returned to find Damien in the sunroom, she'd already caught the shuttle bus back to Winter Park.

"It's not like you to mix business and BDSM," Damien observed, sipping from a glass of mineral water, enhanced with a twist of lime.

David didn't need long to think about that. "If the woman in question wasn't Maggie, it wouldn't have happened tonight."

Damien waited.

"Until now I've never before wanted to paddle someone who reports to me."

"I can understand the temptation."

A house sub accepted David's bag and left them alone without ever saying a word.

"How did it go?" Damien asked.

David frowned. "You tell me. Obviously you saw her before she left, if you knew she was gone."

"I'm afraid you'll have to ask her yourself," Damien said after what seemed to be a considerable silence.

"Fair enough. She was okay, though?"

"It doesn't appear you made her cry."

"Maybe I'm losing my touch."

Damien shrugged. "Or she's tougher than we gave her credit for. At any rate, you needn't worry about her, I'd say."

David knew he'd get nothing more out of Damien. That was something confounding and reassuring about the Den's owner. The man knew everything and revealed no one's confidences. While it could be frustrating, it was reassuring.

From the corner of his eye, David saw Brandy put up her hand to push away a man. "Brandy may need us to intervene."

Damien looked.

Niles, another House Monitor, had obviously already seen what was happening and had moved towards the pair. David wasn't surprised at the other man's quick action, but he was surprised to see Niles at the Den. He hadn't attended many public functions since the death of his beautiful wife and sub.

"I'll handle it," Damien said, following David's gaze. "If you're back on duty, the patio needs an extra set of eyes." He turned away then paused and looked back. "Unless you require a little more time to collect yourself?"

"Not at all." David welcomed the responsibilities. Having something to do suited his personality better than worrying or fretting over Maggie. He was the type of man who shoved aside mental and emotional entanglements. Or he had until Maggie had fled without them having the serious talk they needed.

Confounded woman.

"That's what I expected." With a brisk nod, Damien left.

David took up his post outside near the speaker. Thankfully, Evan C was on hiatus, or whatever a band break was called. David wasn't sure how much more his eardrums could take of that racket. And some people considered it music. Took all kinds.

As it was Ladies' Night, there were dozens of subs inside and outside, all shapes and sizes, all of them appealing in some way, from soft curves to lean lines. Some women he'd seen before. From their behaviour, others were obvious first-timers.

None of them interested him.

It went deeper than the fact he'd recently had sex. But that was where it had to end.

David was a man of his word He intended to keep his end of the deal he'd made tonight with Maggie. He didn't fraternise. He kept his professional boundaries firm so that no employee would try to curry favour. Each week he signed pay cheques, and he didn't want anyone worrying that if they rebuffed an advance or didn't invite him to a party that their job was on the line. Everyone knowing where he stood made life simpler.

Since he didn't socialise much, he spent considerable time by himself.

Not that he minded.

It had taken him a while to admit he was probably better off alone. His ex-wife had called him selfish.

When he'd got married, he'd thought it was forever. He'd never wanted a divorce. Worse, he hadn't seen it coming. One day, six years ago, he'd arrived home from work, hours later than he'd planned. A plate of cold food had been sitting on the table. All of Sandra's belongings had been gone.

It had taken that for him to admit he had an obsessive personality. His single-minded focus on what he wanted excluded everything else in his life.

In the settlement, he'd instructed his lawyer to give Sandra everything she asked for. She'd unselfishly given him six years of her life — she deserved financial compensation as well as the happiness he hadn't provided for her.

He wasn't bitter, he was just wiser. Avoiding relationships was better for the woman, if not for him.

Allowing himself the freedom to think about Maggie for even five minutes would be a bad decision. They'd work together until her employment contract was up, and that would be the extent of their future involvement.

Still, he fingered the handcuffs hanging from his belt loop.

Despite his most powerful intentions, he couldn't help but think about tightening them around her wrists.

He wanted her on her knees and in his cuffs.

Chapter Four

Stark raving mad.

Thoughts of David Tomlinson were going to drive Maggie insane.

Instead of getting out of her car and walking the few blocks to the Market Street offices, she sat there staring at the Rocky Mountains. Even the stunning sight of bright sunshine splashing on the distant peaks couldn't banish images of David from her mind.

Ever since her father had passed when she was ten, Maggie had prided herself on her predictable, responsible behaviour. She'd helped her mother with cooking and cleaning. Maggie had learnt to set an alarm clock and get herself to school. She'd secured a college scholarship and had worked as a waitress so she'd never have to ask her struggling mother for anything.

Even when she was ill, Maggie showed up to work on time to unlock the door. She didn't trust her mother to do it. When ideas were flowing, Gloria often stayed up all night. Even in the best of circumstances, time seemed to be a vague concept to her.

A number of people had keys to the office. David was almost always early. Anyone could open up, but Maggie felt it was her responsibility to be there for the official start of business. So why was she still in the vehicle at ten past eight, fingers curled around the steering wheel?

In her typical fashion, she forced herself to face facts. She was stalling.

At the Den, she'd been filled with bravado. She had promised herself she could strip down, accept a spanking from her boss and finish with him fucking her. Why not? As she'd said, they were both adults. The incident was an interlude in their lives and had no bearing on their work relationship.

When she was dressed, looking at him with his armband and bare chest, she had realised she'd been lying to herself.

The scene had been scorching hot.

Over the years, she'd been with many Doms. Most of them had been fantastically good and had made sure she was satisfied. But David had been focused, pushing her, demanding her full participation.

Feeling conflicted, wanting to pretend it was another in a long series of one-off scenes, but already picturing a continuation, she had tried to leave, only to be stopped by Master Damien. It would have been rude to brush past him, and really, when the house's owner requested a moment, a sub gave it to him, no matter what he or she was dealing with.

He'd looked at her enquiringly and let her know he'd checked on her while she played with Master David.

She'd promised Master Damien she was okay, but she suspected he'd seen through her tremulous smile.

She'd reassured him that David had been a considerate Dom.

After a few more questions, Master Damien had allowed her to leave.

She'd caught the first available bus back to Winter Park. When Vanessa had arrived at the hotel sometime after midnight, she hadn't cared that Maggie was in bed. Instead, Vanessa had flipped on a light, poured them each a glass of wine and demanded to know every last, little detail.

Since they were best friends, they were always there for one another. Therefore, Vanessa had vicariously lived through the whole fiasco with the company's acquisition. Maggie had felt a bit betrayed by her mother's lack of honesty about the firm's financial situation. Because her lax attitude towards bills and collections had put them in a precarious position, Gloria had opened the door to the takeover.

Vanessa had made Maggie see a brighter side, and they'd laughed as they'd painted a picture of David Tomlinson with horns and a pointy tail. More than anyone, Vanessa knew how complex Maggie's relationship was with David.

Upon learning Maggie had just been screwed by the handsome devil-Dom—literally as well as figuratively—Vanessa had bounced on the bed's edge and predicted that Maggie would beg Master David to spank her again, within a fortnight.

Hearing Vanessa call her boss Master David had made Maggie a little dizzy. To her, Master David was a totally different person than the one she worked with and was obligated to. *Wasn't he?*

Maggie wasn't sure how she was going to act towards him today. Cool? Professional? Nonchalant? Or maybe warmer than normal? For certain, she would not behave like a submissive. She'd meet his gaze, talk to him as an equal.

She'd half expected to hear from him yesterday. But the phone had remained silent. Her nerves were taut.

Reminding herself she wasn't a coward, she determinedly unwrapped her hands from the death grip she had on the steering wheel.

She gathered her purse and briefcase, kept her sunglasses on her face to disguise the weekend's lack of sleep then exited and locked the vehicle.

Pretending this was a day like any other, she purposefully walked towards the brick building that housed World Wide Now. As she neared the entrance, her shoulders slumped a little. She could be in denial all she wanted. But most Monday mornings she didn't arrive at the office bearing a welt her boss had left on her ass.

She drew a breath, smoothed her skirt and hair, dropped her sunglasses in her purse then opened the door and stepped inside.

The receptionist sat at the front desk, a huge mug of coffee in front of her.

"Morning, Mags," Barb greeted.

"Tell me there's more of that coffee?" she asked hopefully.

"Are you kidding? I just put on the second pot. Should be about done."

"How long have you been here?"

"Eleven minutes."

Maggie laughed. Good thing coffee went on the office supplies line item in the budget. Mr Tomlinson didn't have to know how much was actually spent on staples and paperclips as opposed to caffeine. "So," she said. "What kind of mood is David in today?"

The receptionist shrugged. "No idea. I haven't seen him yet."

"Meaning he's in his office with the door closed?"

"Meaning he hasn't shown up yet. I was the first one here today."

Maggie blinked. World Wide Now had flexible work hours, except for certain prescheduled meetings. David Tomlinson was a by-the-rules and by-the-clock owner. Employees coming and going at all hours didn't sit well with him and was one of the reasons he often reached for one of the many primary-coloured stress balls that he kept on his credenza. In all the time he'd owned the company, he'd never shown up late.

"He didn't call in or anything." Barb shrugged. "Since he's not here, it's kind of a mini-vacation for us. You should enjoy it."

Maggie felt like a deflated balloon.

It had taken her all morning to psyche herself up, and he wasn't even here?

After getting a much-needed cup of coffee, she headed for her office and slumped into the chair behind her desk.

She checked her emails and voice messages. There was nothing from David, but she had a response from a potential client she'd been trying to schedule a meeting with. She also had a message from their preferred caterer. Maggie and her mother had decided to host an open house as a way to increase business and introduce David to their existing clients. It would keep her busy for a while and, honestly, give her something to fixate on other than her boss spanking her again.

She wished the scene at the Den hadn't met so many of her turn-ons.

Damn.

With determined focus, she sent a list of possible times to the potential new customer, studied the catering menu and made some notes to go over with David, since he now had to approve her budget. An hour later, her coffee was gone, she'd handled all the urgent tasks and she still hadn't heard from her boss.

Her mother, however, showed up in a long, flowing skirt and tank top, with jewellery dripping everywhere — necklaces, bracelets, earrings, even toe rings. She'd obviously dyed her hair over the weekend, and her fingernails were manicured. She looked fresh and radiant and, as she theatrically threw herself into a chair, every inch a creative diva.

"What are you drinking?" Maggie asked, looking at the plastic cup her mother held. The liquid was deep green with chunks of something floating at the surface.

"Green tea latte. With soy."

"Lactose intolerant again?" she asked.

"Still," Gloria corrected.

She hadn't been on Friday when Barb had brought in flavoured cappuccinos with whipped cream on top.

"Where's the tyrant?"

"David?"

"Who else would I be talking about?" Gloria sipped through the straw and wrinkled her nose before schooling her features.

Maggie was betting the green tea phase wouldn't last past Wednesday. "He's not here yet."

"I need his signature on a contract."

With a sigh, Maggie nodded. For so long, it had been just the two of them. Since she'd joined forces with her mother about five years ago, they'd made quick decisions then moved forward. Gloria had signed all the contracts. Between the two of them, they'd handled all the negotiations. Now David double-checked everything, verified the math, set deadlines and reviewed every file. It was time consuming.

But, if Maggie were honest she'd admit that his attention made everything at World Wide Now run smoother than it ever had in the past. Last quarter, they'd posted their first double-digit profit. They had projections of how much profit they'd make per job.

On a daily basis, the staff complained about his interference, but the truth was, the business would have needed to downsize or relocate to a less expensive zip code if he hadn't come along when he had. Her mother might chafe at answering to a man, and a young one at that, but there was no doubt she was now producing her best work.

David Tomlinson believed in exploiting each person's talents. Sometimes that meant assigning them to a new position. In Gloria's case, it meant getting her entirely out of the bookkeeping. She no longer saw bills. Even better, someone else was tasked with handling collections. Getting the financial burden off her shoulders had given her a lot of freedom.

He'd been right to restructure the staff's responsibilities, but she wished her mother's confidence hadn't been undermined by his high-handed ways. Then again, that was probably the only way he knew. The man was assured, directive. Domineering.

"I'd like this contract to go out today," Gloria said.

"Call him?" Maggie suggested, grateful her mother had interrupted her musings.

"Maybe Barb can."

"Mother, he's not an ogre."

"That's the first time I've heard you defend the man."

Was it? Had she really been so swept up in her disdain for the employment contract that she never said anything good about him? "Maybe I need more coffee."

"You do look tired." Gloria narrowed her eyes. "What did you do this weekend, anyway?"

"Went to the Den."

"That explains it. I may have to go with you sometime. Sounds like a kick."

"Why not? Maybe you can find someone to keep you in line, finally."

"On second thought..." With that Gloria stood, creating a cacophony with her clanging metal jewellery.

Just then, David appeared in her doorway.

Maggie's breath vanished in a shocking rush.

He propped his shoulder against the jamb, and he filled the entrance. Damn. She'd spent all of yesterday trying to convince herself he wasn't one of the most handsome men she'd ever seen.

When she'd shut her eyes in bed last night, memories had tormented her. She'd tossed and turned before finally getting up and watching three hours of television.

And now... His dove-grey suit hugged his broad shoulders. His tailored pants snuggled his strong thighs. He had on a white shirt and a red tie with the knot tight. She would greet him, if she could make her tongue work.

"Ladies," he said.

"Good afternoon," Gloria said pointedly.

Since it wasn't even ten o'clock, Maggie winced. For the first time, she wished her mother would at least pretend to be cordial. If they could all work as a team, perhaps the business could reach his lofty goals.

Everyone, including her mother, would benefit from that.

"I need you to sign a contract," Gloria continued.

"Put it on my desk. I'll handle it before anything else."

"But—"

"Put it on my desk, Gloria," he reiterated. He stepped aside.

All but flouncing, she brushed past him.

Without an invitation, he entered Maggie's office and took the seat her mother had vacated.

She wished he hadn't entered her domain. Almost every office on this floor was bigger than hers, and the conference room with its glass wall would be even better.

Here she was, very much on edge. His eyes were as blue as she remembered—intense and deep. That surprised her a little. She was certain her memory was tainted by the scene they'd shared. Surely no one's eyes were that penetrating. But his were.

His scent was slightly different today, though. He still smelt of masculine spice, but it was stamped with confidence that beckoned her to move closer, something she refused to do.

What in the hell had made her think that fucking him was a good idea?

She had to get him out of here, quick, before she asked him to bend her over his chair. "Did you need something...?" Maggie hesitated. Calling him Mr Tomlinson would remind her of the Den. On the other hand, she had never addressed him David at work. Now that he'd compelled her to call her Mr Tomlinson as a term of respect rather than derision, he'd effectively changed the dynamic of their relationship.

He waited.

"Did you need something, David?" she asked.

"I'm in negotiation to acquire another company."

She sat up in her chair. With the solemn expression on his face, she'd expected him to mention what had happened on Saturday night. But he was talking business while she was all but obsessing about the time they'd spent together? Obviously he was better at separating events than she was. She gave herself a mental shake and forced herself to concentrate on what he was saying. "And you're telling me this, why?"

"They're a competitor of ours."

She let out a breath.

"If the deal goes through, it will impact you."

"How so?"

"Your role will grow. I'll need more time from you."

"Good God, no. You've got all you're ever going to get from me." She stiffened her spine.

He propped an ankle on the opposite knee. He looked so corporate, so unconcerned by her response.

"Hear me out," he said.

"There's not much reason for that. If you want to go around buying up businesses in your free time, go right ahead. You and I have a written agreement in place. I have eighteen more months that I'm obligated to help you. Then I'm a free agent. I'm not open to negotiation."

"Everyone has a price, Maggie."

Maggie. At work, he'd always called her Margaret. Until now. It seemed they'd both shown up with a new rule book today.

She twisted her fingers together on top of the desk. Then, seeing he was studying her, noting her betrayal of nerves, she pressed her palms together.

"I'll do whatever it takes to keep you and your talents on the payroll. Of course I'm hoping you'll stay with me because you want to, since we —"

"Excuse me?" Anger, hot, searing, embarrassing, blazed through her. Had he used her? "Was that what Saturday night was about? Part of your plan to manipulate me?"

He dropped his leg to the floor and leant forwards.

"Flog me and fuck me as a way to keep me working for you?" she demanded. "It wasn't enough that you tied my performance to my mother's financial security?"

"If you think that was about anything other than my desire for you as a woman, as a submissive, you're wrong."

His flat statement made her blink. He didn't meet her emotion, he defused it.

She collapsed back in her chair.

"Let's keep things straight, Maggie," he said softly. "When I saw you at the Den in that skirt and those shoes with your hair all around your shoulders…" He trailed off, reached for the door and, with a flick of his wrist, sealed them in intimacy.

She grabbed hold of the chair arms.

"I was intrigued," he continued. "When I saw your wristband, I had to have you. Honestly, I was attracted to you. I would have desired you even if we'd never met. Then with the perfect way you responded to my commands, the way you begged for my touch —"

"That can't happen again."

"It will," he said in a tone that left no other option. "And I'm going to make it very clear to you that fucking, beating, restraining you has nothing to do

with our work relationship." He lowered his voice.
"You want it too."

She hated that he was right. She craved his touch.

"We will discuss that in a few minutes. Here are the
options. I want you to be very much involved in the
acquisition of Around the World in Eighty Ways."

Her mouth dropped. As much as she believed that
was a ridiculous name for a company, their strategy
was similar to World Wide Now's, and they were a
big competitor. For years she'd dreamt of putting
them out of business. And he was offering her the
chance to be part of that. She couldn't let him know
how much the idea appealed to her. "That's
ambitious."

"Everything I do is risky. When I see something I
want, I go after it." He looked at her pointedly. "And
as you know, I don't fail."

She tried to keep her mind on his new proposition,
rather than allowing images of his naked body to fill
her mind. "How will this affect my employment
contract?"

"As I said, it will take a lot of work to get the deal
done. We want to go through their books, assess their
sales projections and year-to-date results. We have to
perform our due diligence. Of course, both sides have
signed non-disclosures."

She nodded. "And we have to keep this business
running at an optimal level while you're distracted."

"Precisely."

"That's where I come in."

"Negotiating the deal is only the beginning."

How well she remembered from the way he'd taken
over her mother's company.

"The first six months will be the most complicated.
We may need to adjust the number of employees. I

need someone who understands strategy and tactics. I need your cooperation and your brain."

"I'm already working enough hours for you as it is, David."

"And that's a hardship, is it, Maggie?"

A little thrill pulsed in her. At one time, it had been.

"As for your employment contract, it stays in place under the original terms."

When she started to speak, he raised a hand to silence her. Snarling against his unspoken demand, she fell silent.

"Unless you agree to my new terms."

"Which are?"

"The time remaining is unchanged."

Beneath her desk, she worried one of her cuticles.

"Assuming you meet the goals I set for you here, your mother's pay-out remains the same, but I'll give you a hundred thousand dollar bonus, after taxes."

She stared at him with open-mouthed shock.

"Interested yet? How about plus ten per cent of all profits of the combined companies?"

The offer was beyond anything she might have asked for. Still, if this worked, he would be the big winner. Of course, he was the one taking all the financial risk. "Gross profit," she clarified.

"In that case, five per cent."

"Ten."

He sat back. "That's not how negotiation works, Maggie. You give a little."

"I learnt from the best." She pretended her heart wasn't racing. This wasn't how she'd expected the day to begin. "Look, David, we both know you'll be taking a loan to buy out AWEW. You could accelerate the debt servicing and take all the profits out of the business. If you want my help, knowing it will take a lot of hours and it will likely take months to get the deal done—time that I will not be paid for—then I need a cut of gross."

"The bonus covers that," he told her.

She took a gamble, ignoring the butterflies unfurling in her stomach. "No deal. I'm happy to stay under my original terms."

He regarded her with those chilling blue eyes.

Since she was accustomed to it, the look shouldn't have unnerved her as much as it did. But now that she'd been the focus of his complete attention on multiple levels, she knew the depths of his intent. He missed nothing, and he thought things through before acting.

"Seven per cent," he told her.

Potentially, that was a lot of money for a year and a half's worth of work. She should take it. But she wasn't going to. "Nine. Final offer."

"Eight."

"Done. And I'll expect this to be added to the contract by tomorrow."

"*Fuck,*" he said.

She wasn't sure she'd heard him use that word in a frustrated way before. In fact, she wasn't sure she'd heard any real inflection in his tone before. She'd only seen him as controlled. This was new. *Intriguing.* "You were serious that you don't like to lose."

"I don't. I'll just have to make sure we both work hard enough to make it a win for each of us." He crossed his leg over his knee again. "You're going to be putting in a lot of time, Maggie."

With him. That part remained unspoken.

"As for the other, I will have you again, Maggie."

She froze.

No matter how insane the idea was, she very much wanted it, too.

"Have a glass of wine with me tonight."

"No."

"No?"

"Let me be honest with you."

"Please."

Ridiculously, as if someone might be watching, she glanced around. "Having a relationship with the boss is a stupid idea. You have rules regarding fraternising. If anyone found out, you could be suspected of manipulating me. I might be accused of sleeping with the enemy."

"And?" he prompted when she trailed off. "There's more," he said with certainty.

She sighed. "If I meet you for a glass of wine, my inhibitions will be loosened. I'll end up naked, and I will beg you to fuck me."

"The scene...it worked for you?"

"I've thought of nothing else. So I'm doing the smart thing by turning down the invitation."

"Are you sure that's what you want?"

"I am." Maggie wondered if he heard the tremor of uncertainty in her voice.

He nodded.

She waited for him to protest or something.

Instead, he stood. "As you wish." With a crisp nod, he exited the room, leaving the door open.

Slack-jawed, she stared at the empty threshold. What the hell had just happened? She felt as if the earth had been knocked off its axis. Was it possible she'd won two battles in a row against David Tomlinson?

She tapped her fingers on the desktop. No. It wasn't likely.

Which had to mean he was changing his strategy. If full-on didn't work, he'd try something else.

The day passed in a blur of activity, including a staff meeting that David didn't attend. In fact, he'd left for lunch around eleven and never returned. To her knowledge, he'd told no one where he was going or when he'd be back. All afternoon, she'd looked over her shoulder, expecting to see him. She'd told herself she wasn't hoping to see him, but a small, constant voice whispered that she was lying.

Feeling somewhat ridiculous, she stayed late on the off chance he might return.

At twenty minutes after five, she determined he wasn't coming back. Even if he did, would it be a good idea to be alone with him? Neediness was crawling through her. Avoiding him was the most sensible course of action.

While she didn't necessarily want to live a twenty-four-seven BDSM lifestyle, she loved everything about the power exchange—giving up control, being subject to a strong Dom's will.

Being with David had given her satisfaction. Resisting him when he was near would be all but impossible. So, she told herself, it was better for her that he hadn't been in the office.

She powered down her computer, turned off her office light then went home.

* * * *

After eating a salad, she poured a glass of wine and went outside to sit on the deck. As she watched, the sky started to turn orange. Shadows hovered over the Rockies, making them look darker and moodier than they had earlier.

Maggie sipped her wine and wondered where David would have taken her if she'd accepted the invitation to join him for a drink. His house? A nice restaurant? Or the new speakeasy that had recently opened to rave reviews on Larimer Street, just a block over from World Wide Now's building? And where would the evening have ended?

Her place? His?

Now that she'd stopped moving, unwelcome thoughts caught up to her.

She admired his ambition in wanting to acquire a competitive business. But she wasn't sure she relished the idea of spending even more time with him. The more time they spent together, the more she'd be tempted to scene with him. It was better for her not to be alone with him in the first place.

The wine hadn't taken off the edge—in fact it seemed to exacerbate her internal angst.

She headed back inside to take a shower then set the tap to scalding, as if it would help exorcise the tension she was feeling.

While she stood there, the memories she'd been shoving away caught her and held her enthralled. The harder she tried to fight them, the deeper their grip became.

She closed her eyes and saw herself tied to the table, spread for him as he explored her body. Resolve crumbled. She remembered the feel of his fingers as he toyed with her clit then entered her body.

Maggie reached for the showerhead and detached it from its hook.

After adjusting the setting from spray to pulse, she directed the water over her body, letting it pummel her nipples before going lower. She spread her legs and parted her labia.

She imagined he was there with her, touching her, making her squirm.

His rich voice seemed to resonate in her ears, and she could hear him urging her to hold on, to wait, to surrender.

She moved her hips, seeking more sensation on her swollen clit. She was ready to come, wanted the orgasm.

Imagining him urging her on, she screamed and climaxed, dropping the showerhead and grabbing onto a bar for support.

It took a full minute for her to regain control. She forced herself to uncurl her clenched fingers and finish her shower.

Damn, he'd got into her head.

Generally when she had fantasies, the Dom was nameless and faceless. But this time, it had been so much more real, as if he'd been there with her.

A powerful orgasm always helped relax her, but this time, it left her feeling more restless, maybe because she realised she wasn't able to forget about David.

It took over an hour of tossing and turning before she finally fell asleep.

She was hunted in her dreams, chased by an overwhelming force. She was running down the street, desperate for breath. Finally, a hand landed on her shoulder, spinning her around. She screamed and screamed, and when she faced it, she saw a pulse of electric blue. When she reached up to shove it — him — away, the spectre vanished.

With a start, she woke up, drenched in sweat.

Shaking, she climbed from her bed. She grabbed a robe and wrapped the belt around her waist, cinching it tight. After turning on every light in the house, she grabbed a glass of water and headed outside.

Some college students were hanging out on another patio, drinking beer and having more fun than she was.

She realised she'd only ever seen that shade of blue in one place. David Tomlinson's eyes.

Damn it.

How the hell was she supposed to survive working even more closely with him?

Her mind was in a battle with her body. Though she craved his touch, she was smart enough to recognise the emotional threat he posed. But that didn't stop her from wanting, desperately wanting.

Maggie leaned against the railing and glanced at the sky. The moon was obscured by some clouds but the normality helped to stop her hand from trembling.

Determined to relegate him to the position of boss and nothing larger in her life, she went back to bed. The rest of the night was fitful, and the alarm rang way too early.

Exhausted, she dressed all in black, donning it as if it were armour. Her relationship with David did feel a bit like a battle. He was a master strategist, and she was always a step behind.

"Morning, Mags." Barb glanced around then whispered, "The tyrant is here."

Maggie's heart lurched. She wanted to see him, and equally she needed to avoid him. The remnants of last night's dream haunted her. "Oh?"

"He's brewing coffee. I asked if he needed help, but he said he thinks he can handle it." Barb shrugged. "I'm not sure I believe he's capable of menial tasks. Maybe one of us should make sure he's not screwing up."

At one time, Maggie might have added a disparaging comment of her own. She was learning he was more complex than she'd originally given him credit for, but that didn't mean she planned to organise the David Tomlinson fan club anytime soon. "I'm on it," Maggie said.

He was wiping down the counter when Maggie entered the break room.

She had seen him organise his toys at the Den. Here, however, wearing a suit coat and tie, he looked out of place.

"I was sent to ensure you know what you're doing."

"Oh?" Still holding a towel, he turned to look at her.

"This is serious." She fought to hide a smile. "The productivity of the entire business rests on your shoulders."

"I gathered that from Barb's reaction, so I dumped as much coffee in the filter as it would hold, and I filled the tank to the top."

She glanced at the pot then back at him. "We should be okay," she said. "As long as you used a new filter? Sometimes people put new grounds on top of old ones."

"I thought about it," he said. He moved to look at her. "It seems the basket didn't get cleaned out last night, so the temptation was there. But as you say, productivity is at stake. I figured the more caffeine the better. Cost analysis weighed towards the extra scoops."

"Good call."

They exchanged grins.

His smile dissipated as he looked at her, starting at her shoes and working his way up.

She stood there, riveted.

When their gazes met, she shuddered. His eyes were the same startling blue as in her nightmare, throwing her back into the memory and making her wary.

"I spent all of last night thinking about holding you down."

Breathless. He left her breathless.

He laid the towel across the dish drain. "My office? Fifteen minutes? We need to talk about Around the World."

How did he do that? Flip from sex to business in three seconds? "That should be enough time for me to check messages," she said.

He nodded and moved past her.

Maggie wondered how much time he spent dreaming up ways to keep her off kilter.

After depositing her purse and briefcase in her office, checking voicemail and emails, she returned to the break room to grab a cup of coffee. Barb was already happily sipping hers. The receptionist had added so much flavoured creamer that it looked like a latte and smelt like vanilla ice cream.

Maggie poured herself a cup then paused. David's mug was on the counter, waiting to be filled. She waged an internal debate before getting one for him.

She carried both to his office. Seeing he was on a call, she stopped, but he waved her in.

He continued his conversation while keeping his gaze on her.

Self-consciously, she placed his mug on a coaster bearing the company's logo. Then she balanced her cup as she sat.

She started to fidget then, realising what she was doing, she crossed her legs and sat still.

He nodded, letting her know his attention was on her.

She looked away.

Behind him, on a credenza, were several stress balls, each in a different primary colour. Other than that, there were no personal effects in the office. He'd repainted after her mother had moved out—evidently bright yellow didn't suit him.

Now the walls were a calm taupe. The furnishings were sleek and functional, with no space wasted and nothing cluttered.

She wondered if it was a reflection of him, and how he lived his life outside of work. Really, she knew little about him. Until now, she hadn't been curious.

When he hung up, he said, "I saw you behave similarly at the Den. Once you recognise your behaviour, you correct it. It makes you a very good sub."

"Could we not talk about that night? I thought we agreed not to." She looked at him, desperately trying to forget the dream and about the night they'd shared.

"As you wish, Maggie. Thanks for the coffee."

"My pleasure," she said, fighting a compulsion to add an honorary title when she spoke to him. How did he so effortlessly do that? Put her in a comfortable role and make her want to stay there. She wondered who she was fighting, him or herself.

He took a drink and regarded her above the rim.

She waited for him to speak, after all, he'd requested her presence.

"I had meetings with the owner and a key manager of Around the World yesterday."

"And?"

"We went over their financials. They are not as big as we are."

"Are you serious? I was sure they did more revenue."

"More business," he agreed. "But they've underbid some of their bigger projects."

"So that should put you—" She stopped and corrected herself—"I mean us, in a better position."

"We should get an immediate lift in profits, yes. But raising prices could mean losing some accounts."

"You don't sound worried about it."

"I'm not. I focus on results and the things I can control." He put down his coffee. "Where are we on the open house?"

"Do you still want to move forward?"

"I thought about that. I do. No sense putting it off. I still want an event with our current clients. And it makes sense to have something bigger and splashier when we own Around the World."

He'd said when, not if.

"Maybe around the holidays," he added.

She thought about it. "We could hold that at a client site. We recently signed a winery. They have beautiful grounds, including a gazebo, and they give tours of their cellar. I think hosting an event there would be elegant, and it would give them some exposure."

He nodded thoughtfully. "Is the space big enough?"

"They have an events centre, yes."

"Ah, it is in Denver?"

She leant forwards, gaining enthusiasm. "Surprisingly yes."

"I'll trust you. Give me some available dates."

"Are we keeping our company name, or are you changing it?"

"We'll stay with our name. But I figure we'd incorporate their logo."

She nodded. "We may want to freshen it. I'll come up with a few ideas, but since this is still quiet, I won't have our graphics people work on it yet." She knew their logo had an eagle of sorts on it. She'd always thought it was a little uninspired, so the idea of tweaking it appealed to her. "We could stick with an eagle, perhaps with talons extended to visually reinforce the 'Now' part of our name."

He nodded. "I like it."

"Maybe I'll see if we can get a privately labelled wine for the occasion. Could serve as the debut of the new marketing package."

"We have a lot of details to plough through before we're close enough to have that discussion," he cautioned.

"You're not the only one who can move fast, David."

He sat back. "Glad we're on the same side."

"It's temporary," she assured him.

"So you say."

* * * *

For the next couple of weeks, Maggie managed to keep her distance, sending emails and text messages to keep him updated on her projects and deals in progress. Their meetings were generally held with other people in the conference room.

He'd honoured her request to stop talking about the night at the Den, and that frustrated her more than his reminders had.

She felt as if she were tied in emotional knots.

Almost every night, she had the same nightmare — the heavy hand on her shoulder and the shock of blue when she was spun around.

She was becoming more and more frustrated from lack of sleep.

Masturbating wasn't helping, and neither was going to the gym.

Finally, almost a month after the Ladies' Night at the Den, she and Vanessa met for dinner. Sushi and sake could fix nearly anything, or at least it had been able to until now.

"Colour me shocked," Vanessa said as she used a chopstick to smear wasabi on a tuna roll. "You're working with one of the world's sexiest Dom's and he's hot for your ass. So tell me again why you can't sleep with him?"

"Hello? He's a bastard who has my future mapped out for the next eighteen months. I can't look for another job. I feel as if my life is on hold."

"I don't get it. Are you not capable of sleeping with a guy without it interfering with your job performance?"

She had no idea. "He has a no fraternising rule."

"So break it and give him something to punish you for."

"Would you be serious here?" Maggie exclaimed.

"Maggie, Maggie, Maggie. You need to relax before you give yourself an ulcer. Fine. He has a policy. Is it in writing in the employee handbook?"

"No."

"Not all companies have those kinds of policies in place, but when they are, it's generally to protect morale, avoid conflicts of interest or to protect subordinates from feeling like they might be harassed. It helps companies avoid sexual harassment charges, but c'mon, Mags, CEOs even marry their executives."

Not only was Vanessa a good friend, she'd spent a number of years working in human resources.

"Your situation is unique," Vanessa continued. "This isn't legal advice, but I'd say that a relationship between the two of you is just that. Unless one of you is going to file a lawsuit, then it's really just personal preference. A lot of small firms employ family members, and this is no worse than you working for your mom. If he's made it clear he's interested in you, then it means he sees you as an equal and not a subordinate. So if you want to fuck him, and he's not using his position of authority to unduly manipulate you, then fuck him." She poured a small amount of soy sauce over the top of the roll then slammed down the bottle and scowled. "*Is* he pressuring you?"

Maggie shook her head. "He hasn't mentioned it in over two weeks. And he's offered me more incentive to stay."

"Have you considered he's just as tied up by that damned contract as you are?"

She took a drink of her cooling sake.

"He's got all his capital invested in your mother's company. He can't go hire a hotshot salesperson who's loyal to him while he's agreed to pay your salary and put money aside for Gloria. Something's gotta give." Vanessa popped the roll in her mouth then blinked furiously.

"Too much wasabi?" Maggie asked with a laugh. The way Vanessa's eyebrows had shot up ruined her lecture and the moment.

"Shit." Vanessa reached for the sake and took a massive gulp. "I need to take it easy here." She fanned herself. "Let me tell you how I see it," she said after dabbing her eyes with a napkin. "You look like hell. You're not sleeping. You're having nightmares. What would happen if you told him the truth?"

Or was it herself she needed to be honest with?

"You've always gone after the things you wanted. You've never been one to let life pass you by. Why start now?"

Maggie thought about that for the rest of the night. Saturday seemed to drag. She finished her laundry and workout by nine o'clock, leaving a yawning gap in her calendar. Vanessa had a date that evening, and her mother was camping out at a music festival. Finally, she considered going to the Den.

The online calendar showed that tonight's event was designed for new Dommes and those interested. It was possible she'd find a dominant male there, but it was a long drive for that gamble.

Truthfully, she wanted another taste of David's lash. It wasn't just a scene she wanted. It was him.

She ended up doing a ton of work from home and streaming an entire season's worth of a police drama. Too often, she wondered what David was doing.

By Sunday, she knew she had to face her nightmare. She wasn't running from him as much as she was trying to protect herself.

That left only one course of action. She had to talk to him.

* * * *

Monday crawled. Since she didn't want to mix work and sex, she decided to talk to him after everyone else had gone home.

Finally, later than normal, her mother waved goodnight, saying she was heading to her first belly dancing lesson. Once the front door had closed, Maggie squared her shoulders and walked down the hallway to David's office.

She knocked on the doorframe and waited until he looked up from the stack of papers before him. "May I come in?"

"Please."

Her stomach plunged as she took a seat. Now that she was here, the object of his scrutiny, she wasn't sure what to say.

He allowed the silence to grow before asking, "Something on your mind, Maggie?"

"I..." She tipped back her head.

Waiting silently, with the patience it took for water to wear a hole in a rock, he reached for a yellow stress ball that was sitting on his desktop.

After swallowing her nerves, she seized all her courage and met his intense gaze. "What does a girl have to do to get a spanking around here?"

Chapter Five

David squeezed the ball tight.

Maggie had asked her question with a light, teasing tone, likely so that she could be flippant about it if he turned her down. But he heard the shakiness that sketched across her vocal chords. Her body was rigid, her smile false and the atmosphere seemed charged with tension. His answer and this moment, both mattered to her.

He'd given up hope that she would mention playing with him again.

And he respected that. If Maggie wanted to keep their personal experience confined to a one-night stand at the Den... Well, that wasn't the way he preferred it, but he wouldn't push. For any relationship with a sub to be successful, she had to offer herself freely. Now that she was here...

He tried not to let her know how many times he'd jacked off, thinking about her coming to him and asking to scene. Since the night at the Den, he'd thought about little else other than Maggie and her unrehearsed responses, her whimpers, the way she moved her body, sometimes with sensuous grace, sometimes with an exaggerated tease.

Part of him realised it would have been smarter not to have played with her in the first place. The taste had whetted his appetite. Seeing her every day, tight skirt clinging to her rounded derrière, made it worse. He'd spent days fantasising about having her in his cuffs, over his knee, under his control.

With deliberate mastery, he reined in his thoughts. Choosing his words with great care, he said, "If a particular sub wanted something, she'd ask, and she'd be specific about her intent." He leant back in his chair and regarded her, deciding how to proceed. He wanted her to feel as if she had some power, but he knew she wanted him to be in charge.

Maggie unclasped her hands and scooted back in the chair, crossing one leg over the other in a sexy slide of silk. Her posture and the way she folded her hands in her lap was perfect.

He adored women who embraced their softer side, but he'd never seen it so integrated in a woman he'd once suspected was a Domme. A tendril of hair had escaped its confines to tease her cheekbone. He wanted to stroke it back as he grabbed her chin and held it hostage. "She would also be frank about her expectations and what she was willing to give. She'd have to be honest with herself as well as me." He released the ball.

"That's what my friend Vanessa told me. That's why I'm here."

He waited, giving her time to sort it through.

"The truth is I haven't slept well in weeks. I think that hooking up with you will relieve some of my angst."

"You just caused permanent injury to my ego, Maggie." He placed his hand over his heart in mock affront. "I was hoping you were going to flatter me, throw yourself on your knees at my feet, telling me I'm a fabulous Dom as you prettily beg for my attention."

She grinned. "That, too."

For a moment, he was silent. This was one of the rare moments of lightness between them and he appreciated it. "The last time we spoke about this, you were clear that you don't want to feel as if I'm manipulating you. Or that you're sleeping with the enemy."

She ran her thumb across a cuticle and didn't seem to know she was doing it.

Again he waited while she picked her words. "If we are both determined to keep our work and our private lives separate, it should work."

"Go on."

"I thought we could scene every once in a while. Get kinky. No strings. Just when it's convenient for both of us. If it suited you, we could meet at the Den and keep it less complicated."

"I can understand if you need that for security."

"I don't."

"In that case, it's easier if we use one of our places."

She nodded.

"When were you wanting to get together?"

"I was hoping we could do it tonight," she admitted. "So that I can sleep. I understand if —"

"Would you like me to take you for a glass of wine first to loosen your inhibitions?"

"I don't need anything else from you."

"Any more ways you'd like to destroy my ego?"

"You asked for honesty," she reminded him with a charming, fake smile. "So, what do you say? You gonna spank me or not?"

"I'll give you a ten minute head start while I finish up a few things here. When I arrive at your place, I want you naked, lying on your back on the floor, your knees raised and held apart by your hands. Any questions?"

"Where in the house? My bedroom?"

"You tell me."

"Ah..." She shifted. "Right inside the doorway."

"Good answer. I'll need your address." He slid a piece of paper across to her.

Maggie scooted forwards on her chair and wrote down her information.

"I'll be right behind you," he reminded her.

She looked at him. Her brown eyes were wide, unblinking, and her lips were slightly parted.

He'd yet to touch her, but because of the things he'd said, he knew the scene was already in progress. His cock hardened as she stood and smoothed the front of her skirt, like he'd seen her do at the Den. The betrayal of her nerves was utterly feminine and enchanting.

She paused at the door and looked back over her shoulder. He waited patiently. A few seconds passed.

Saying nothing, she left.

David finished his work, shut down his computer, turned off the lights and walked through the offices, giving her the allotted amount of time.

His car was the last one in the parking lot. As he climbed behind the wheel of the German sedan, he saw the handcuffs that he had left on the console. The metal glinted in the sunlight. Before the night was out, he'd have her in them.

He navigated out of the maze of one-way streets and merged onto the crowded interstate. Restlessness and anticipation collided. He'd be there soon enough. The more time he gave her to get ready for him, the better.

Ever since their night together, he'd been unable to get thoughts of her out of his mind. He hoped she knew how much he, too, wanted this. It had been years since he'd had a regular playmate. He wondered if Maggie had felt the same constraints at the Den that he experienced. The pleasure that came with exploring a new woman was gratifying, but to him, getting to know a sub—figuring out her likes, catering to them, finding her limits and shattering them—was even more rewarding.

That the sub was Maggie...

He admired her courage in coming to him. All too well, he understood the restlessness she spoke of. Sex was the ultimate stress reliever for him, and being buried deep inside her body satisfied him in a way that jacking off never would.

The understanding they had in place to protect their work agreement was even more freeing. And neither of them seemed interested in anything more. Sceneing together on a semi-regular basis could fit the bill nicely for both of them.

He exited the highway on the south end of the metro area, and as he drove west, the traffic thinned out. It was a bonus that she lived in the same general direction as his house in Castle Rock.

Her condo complex had nicely tended gardens and an inviting-looking swimming pool. As for the hot tub, the one in his backyard was much more private.

He attached the cuffs to his belt loop and took the steps up to the second floor to find her place.

After knocking once, he tried the knob and found it unlocked.

He let himself in and secured the deadbolt behind him.

As he'd instructed, she was lying on her back on the living room floor, legs spread, knees held apart. Her chest rose and fell rapidly. Maggie was stunning in her nudity and compliance. His cock hardened at the sight. The weeks of waiting had been worth it.

"Beautiful," he murmured as he walked around her, looking at her from every angle. She'd closed the blinds and, he presumed, moved a coffee table up against a wall.

Her space was what he'd expected—spare, sleek, modern and conservative, a reflection of her. She had few knickknacks, and the two paintings on the walls were slashes of bold, abstract colour. "I love the way your pussy is on such perfect display for me. Since you're so well behaved, I may go a little easier on you than planned." That was a lie. He'd give her everything she asked for, and more. "Would you like me to start by pulling your nipples until you cry out?"

She exhaled a shaky breath.

He crouched next to her and kept her gaze hostage as he flicked her right nipple several times until it became a hard peak. "Hmm?"

"Yes, please, Mr Tomlinson."

"That's what you like, isn't it, sub?"

"Oh yes. It is."

He stood long enough to shrug out of his suit jacket and drape it over the back of the couch. Then he rolled back his cuffs before squatting again. Since he knew she was expecting him to play with her nipples, he stunned her by smacking her gorgeous cunt.

Maggie arched her back and cried out.

"Do you need a gag?" He didn't wait for a response. Instead, he loosened his tie, pulled it from around his neck then wadded it and said, "Open your mouth."

When she did, he shoved the material between her teeth. "That's meant to give you a bit more freedom to scream, but your hands are free. Remove it if you need to use your slow word. Eclipse, right?" He waited for her assent before continuing. "Halt will stop the action right away. Or touch me. I'll be watching you and your reactions, regardless. I'll try to make sure we don't go too far, but we haven't played together enough for me to know your exact preferences."

She nodded.

Next time, he'd arrange for her to visit his house — there were no neighbours nearby, so she could be as loud as she liked. The higher the volume, the more he'd enjoy the experience. "I want you to do your best to keep your legs apart."

She mumbled something that sounded like agreement.

"Release your knees and keep your hands flat against the floor unless you need to signal me." He stroked her heated pussy. She held herself rigid, as if bracing for his next smack. He was more calculating than to provide what she expected. He wanted to know her every reaction, but he didn't intend to telegraph his intentions.

He made soothing sounds while he slid his fingers on the inside of her labia. She drew a deep breath and exhaled, allowing her body to relax. She seemed to allow the floor to take more of her weight, and her body's response coated his fingers with moisture. "That's it." He continued until he knew she was almost orgasmic, then he smacked her again, hard, three times in rapid succession.

Panting, she looked up at him.

To her credit, she stayed in position. "Do you like that, Maggie?"

She nodded.

"Perfect." It was a treat to be with a woman whose desires matched his. "I want you to orgasm from this."

She tightened her buttocks but didn't protest or use a safe signal.

He cupped his hand and slapped her damp pussy several times. She thrashed her head back and forth.

He paused.

When her breathing fell into a more regular pattern, he licked two of his fingers then stroked her again.

She moaned.

"That's it," he soothed. "Give me your responses." David tormented her until she dug her heels into the floor and lifted her hips. He responded by slapping her several more times.

Behind the makeshift gag, she screamed.

He watched her carefully to ensure his repeated blows weren't more torturous than enjoyable.

Deliberately he alternated the teasing and the pain.

She held nothing back, arching to meet his hand.

He smacked her swollen pussy hard.

She took a shuddering breath and lowered her buttocks to the floor. He caressed her, sliding a finger into her pussy.

Then she lifted her pelvis again, signalling her need to continue. "Brave sub," he said, resuming his smacks.

Her pussy became redder.

"Beautiful sight," he told her. "I'm imagining it will still look like this when you're getting ready for work tomorrow. Skip the panties," he said.

She met his gaze. Her eyes were wide.

He wouldn't know if she'd taken his suggestion. But the idea of her labia being plump and tender would distract him all day.

With alternate tenderness and roughness, he brought her to the brink of a climax. "Show me you want it."

She rubbed herself against his hand, arching, seeking.

He made sounds, encouraging her. He met her next thrust, plunging two fingers inside her to find her G-spot and push against it.

David watched her dig her heels into the carpet and saw her legs quiver. He felt her convulse as an orgasm claimed her.

"Ride it," he encouraged.

She moved her hips and groaned.

David grinned, glad she'd come to him. This beat the hell out of a cold beer and booting up his work computer.

When she settled again, he stood and looked at her. Her skin was covered with a fine sheen of dampness.

Her curvy body lay open for him. She had given him the power to both give and withhold pain and pleasure as he saw fit.

It was intoxicating what she'd done to him. Anxious to continue, he asked, "Where are your nipple clamps?"

She inclined her head to indicate a different room.

"Show me." He stood and leant down to offer her a hand. As she slid her palm against his, he was struck by how small she was next to him. It was easy to forget. Her presence demanded respect.

In her bare feet, she didn't reach his chin. She had to tip her head back to look at him. The reminder of her trust and submissiveness humbled him and made him even more determined to please her.

The musk of her arousal smelt sharp on the summer air. It was a good thing he was still dressed, otherwise he would have pinned her to the floor and fucked her hard. "Hands behind you."

Her gaze was riveted to him as she watched him detach the formidable-looking metal from his belt loop.

"I've kept them in the car for you." He moved around to secure them at the small of her back. He checked the position of her shoulders. "Comfortable enough?"

After she nodded, he ratcheted the cuffs one notch tighter. "Turn your thumbs down if you need to signal me. I will be watching you." The sight of the unyielding metal against her creamy skin appealed to him on every carnal level. "You were meant for these, Maggie."

The tie kept her from responding. That was probably a good thing for both of them. Absently he wondered if he could gag her at the office. It would make his life much more pleasant. But, he had to admit, less productive, as well. He'd spent a lot of days fantasising about filling her mouth with other things. "After you," he said.

She hesitated, so he pinched her right buttock, urging her forwards. He followed a couple of steps behind, admiring the way her body swayed seductively as she walked. Her gait was much more feminine than it was at work, as if being naked, cuffed and gagged changed not only her frame of mind but also how she moved her body.

This woman was a natural submissive.

And for now, *his* submissive.

Inside the bedroom, she stopped.

He appreciated that the room was large and uncluttered. There was an en-suite bathroom, and he took a moment to close the blinds and turn on the overhead fan.

She led him towards a small dresser in the closet.

All of her items were well organised. Work clothing was on the far left, grouped by colour. Next she had casual clothing. Then the sexy stuff. He tried not to be distracted by the short skirts, skimpy V-necked blouses and... Jesus. A corset.

He reminded himself to focus. There'd be plenty of time to see her in that garment. He looked forward to cinching her into it.

The first drawer he opened contained her lingerie. He picked up a lacy shelf bra and held it as he looked over his shoulder at her. "Is this what you wear to work?"

She nodded.

"And this?" he asked, scooping up a garter belt.

Even with the tie in her mouth, she managed a grin.

"Every day?" When she nodded, he slammed the drawer closed, knowing he'd never again concentrate at the office. His fingers would be itching to trace the seductive straps that attached to her silky hose. Now that he'd discovered this secret, keeping their work and private lives separate was going to be far more difficult than he'd imagined, especially once he factored in her reddened pussy and soon-to-be tormented buttocks. "I'm going to buy you some granny panties," he said. "And all-day support bras. There's nothing wrong with cotton."

She drew her eyebrows together.

"Maybe a chastity belt."

He found her toys in the next drawer down. As he now expected, everything was in perfect order. She had an organiser to separate each item. Clamps were in one place. Two floggers were laid length-wise across the back. Beneath them was a paddle with holes in it. She also had a hairbrush and a tawse stamped with an eagle. "A Master Marcus creation, if I'm not mistaken?"

Her response was muffled.

"You do like your spankings," he said.

She also had a selection of butt plugs, vibrators and dildos. "Good God, woman." Her treasure trove rivalled his. It would take days to explore how she liked each used. "We're spending the weekend together." He didn't ask if she had plans. If she did, she'd be rescheduling them.

David tested a set of clamps on his smallest finger. "Too lightweight," he surmised, glancing at her.

Her nod confirmed his guess.

The second set was a bit more intense. "You have them laid out by pressure?"

She glanced away as if embarrassed.

"Smart," he said. "Makes it easier to find exactly what you want. Do you want the hardest ones?"

She wrinkled her nose.

As much as he liked having her gagged, they needed to be able to communicate. He removed the tie from her mouth, but he laid it on her shoulder for easy access.

She licked her lips and he was gripped by the image of that tongue pressed against his dick.

With determination, he focused on her.

"I almost never play with the hardest ones," she told him. "I have to work up to them or be really deep into a scene."

"Understood." He selected those and the pair next to them. "These?"

"My favourites," she said.

He tried the pressure. To him, the bite felt vicious. Then he recalled he'd added weights when he'd clamped her at the Den. "Do you need anything before we continue? A drink of water? To stretch your muscles?"

She waited a moment. He expected her to ask for another orgasm or to get on with the spanking, but her silence made it clear she was going to let him set the pace.

"No, Mr Tomlinson. I'm fine. Thank you."

He didn't wait any longer. He picked up the tie and guided her back into the middle of the bedroom.

After depositing the clamps and tie on the nightstand, he captured her right breast and held it while he teased her nipple with his tongue. When it started to lengthen and thicken, he sucked on it.

Maggie moaned and leaned in towards him. Again he was struck by the lack of inhibition in her reactions. Here, she didn't try to hide anything from him. Her little sounds drove him on.

He moved to her left breast and coaxed the same response from her body before pulling back to look at her pretty pink nipples. He adored the way both stood so erect, waiting for his further attention. David pulled on each in turn, elongating them and holding them distended while he placed the clamps.

For a moment, she kept her eyes closed, but when she opened them, she looked at him and said, "Thank you."

Her words sounded heartfelt.

She seemed like a puzzle, each piece unique and complex. To him, she was no longer a woman who worked with him, alternately helpful and confounding, or a sub he enjoyed playing with. She was much more complicated.

He stood and curved his hands around her upper arms. "This is more than a desire for an occasional kick for you, isn't it?"

She drew a few, shuddering breaths.

The silence stretched for so long he began to wonder if she would answer.

"Yes, Mr Tomlinson, it is."

He wanted to know much, much more about her. Watching her, he fisted the chain that draped between her breasts and dragged her nipples together. She gasped but didn't protest. She closed her eyes. There was no anguish on her face, only a calm serenity. "Beautiful," he told her. He eased the pressure.

"Thank you, Mr Tomlinson."

"I do love good manners. How would you like your spanking?"

"Well done," she said cheekily.

He gave her clamps a quick tug.

She sighed.

"Incorrigible wench," he said with an exaggerated huff.

"I liked that," she told him. "The unexpected. It's different when I play with myself. Not knowing what you're going to do, how it's going to feel, being unable to brace myself. To be honest, Mr Tomlinson, it doesn't matter. If it pleases you to continue as you were earlier, that's fine with me. Over the knee works. Or there's a reason I bought a four-poster bed."

Since he'd had her across his lap at the Den, he thought he'd go for something else, though if he were honest, he'd admit that he loved the feel and the sight of her body as she squirmed against his skin. "I'm going to readjust your cuffs." He released the lock and freed one wrist. He rubbed her skin because he wanted the connection he got from touching her. "They don't seem as if they were too tight."

"Not at all."

He massaged her shoulders as well before instructing, "Kneel on the edge of the bed with your ass in the air."

Her motions were deliberate, slow and feminine. As he'd started giving orders, her breathing pattern had changed in response. "Tits on the mattress, Maggie. That's it. I want your breasts to feel those clamps. Ah, yes. Now arch your back a bit more. Show me that beautiful butt." He waited while she followed his instruction. "I should take a picture," he said. "Can't think of a nicer screen saver."

"I hope it would be a distraction," she responded.

"The ultimate. Everything about you is." Including the fact she hadn't protested his idea. He walked around to the far side of the bed. "Give me your wrists, please."

She stayed in the position he'd ordered her into, and she could only lift her head a few inches to look at his eyes as she stretched her hands towards him. Her eyelids were lowered a bit, and he was recognising the look as one that came over her when she was getting deeper and deeper into a submissive headspace.

He secured the cuffs and checked the fit. He held her gaze. "I'm going to beat you," he informed her, "and give you another well-deserved orgasm."

"Thank you, Mr Tomlinson."

"Are you comfortable enough?"

"Not at all."

He grinned. "Perfect."

"I figured that might be your response, Mr Tomlinson."

"Do you really want it otherwise?"

"No," she said clearly.

"As I thought." He moved behind her.

He trailed his fingers down her back until he was between her buttocks. She parted her legs to give him greater access.

He saw the tension in her muscles as she fought to keep herself in place while he fondled her pussy. He continued to touch and explore.

"Please, please, please," she said, now shamelessly pressing against his hand.

The tang of her arousal rent the air and urged him on in a primal need for possession. "How do you keep this side of yourself hidden at work?" He gave her a few light slaps.

"Oh, Mr Tomlinson. That's... It's too..." she said as she wriggled, keeping her butt high.

"You're a bit sensitive from earlier?"

"Yes. It won't take much for me to come. I thought I should let you know."

"I'm glad you did." He changed the tempo to give her momentary respite. "Will the spanking be more memorable to you if you don't orgasm?"

"Probably," she admitted.

"Better not take the chance, hmm?"

"As you wish, Mr Tomlinson."

"I could listen to you say that all day long." After another stroke — because he could — he removed his hand. "Shall I choose the implement? Or is there something you prefer?"

"We'll go with Dom's choice."

"Another good answer, Maggie." She might not have got the hang of the whole respect thing at work, but when her clothes came off, so did her bad attitude.

She settled deeper into the mattress and into herself.

At some point, the only thing he wanted her to wear was a handprint.

He unbuckled his belt and pulled it free from the loops with a snap. She moved in response to the sound, perhaps preparing herself for the first blow.

David folded the leather over and gripped the buckle. She swayed as he spread his legs and turned sideways to her so that he could aim and hit with good, precise swings.

He caught her ass with a vicious smack, and the crack reverberated from the ceiling.

Her sigh flowed over him, filled with the softness of her satisfaction.

She stayed in position and he began the beating in earnest. He caught each of her ass cheeks in turn then landed a powerful blow beneath the curve of her buttocks.

Unlike earlier, she kept quiet, not requiring anything to muffle her sounds.

"You're made for this."

"Yes, Sir."

He fell into a harsh, regular rhythm, bringing back his arm and blazing the leather across her tender skin.

The harder he hit, the more she seemed to relax.

With a hiss of leather, he caught her hard, just above the backs of her knees.

Her head came up a little. A moment later, she said, "Thank you, Mr Tomlinson."

He landed a second on top of it. While he didn't intend to bruise her, that part of her legs would ensure a different position when she sat in her work chair for the next day or so.

"Damn. That's good. More."

David changed his stance and flicked out the belt so it was a single tail. Now he could use the end to catch her skin with the vicious licks she asked for.

She whimpered when he marked her, filling him with the masculine urge to give his woman what she was asking for.

"Please spread your knees farther apart." Once she had, he continued, able to reach more of her unmarred and tender places.

Her noises became a little more pronounced, especially when he lighted across her cunt. "Such a good pet," he murmured.

"Oh, Mr Tomlinson."

"Is that a request for me to slow down?"

"No."

"Or the gag?"

"If it pleases you, Sir. But it's not necessary. Just, please, more."

He resumed his hits, most of them across her buttocks punctuated by an occasional and careful tease of her pussy.

She grabbed the bedding, bunching the comforter in her fingers. The sight of her, exposed and helpless for him, filled him with an intoxicating mixture of power and humility.

Driven by her greed, he measured his spanks, delivering them at the same interval until her sounds all but ceased and she relaxed her grip. He knew she was getting lost in the endorphins flooding her system, but she had the presence of mind to keep her body in the position he'd commanded.

Though his arm was tired, he stayed with her a few more minutes. "I'm going to bring you back," he said, his words a whisper so as not to shatter her reverie. He continued to let the belt fall, but he used less and less force. "Take your time," he said. "I won't hurry you."

He touched her shoulder, then stroked down her spine.

It took at least a full minute for her to begin to move. "That's it," he soothed, tossing the belt on nightstand. The buckle hit with a thud that startled her. "I'm going to release your cuffs," he said with reluctance, remembering the way she'd run after their night at the Den. This time, he wouldn't allow her to put immediate emotional or physical distance between them.

He moved to open the cuffs. As he had earlier, he rubbed her wrists. This time, she was chafed from the metal. "Stay there," he told her. "Please." He crossed to the master bath and washed his hands. He found towels in a cupboard, and he dampened one before carrying it back to her.

Her body was heated and covered in a sheen of perspiration.

His strokes were gentle as he wiped her shoulders, lifted her hair to cleanse her nape then moved lower to give relief to the welts on her buttocks and legs.

"That feels good. Thank you, Mr Tomlinson."

He finished by dabbing her pussy and ass before tossing aside the towel and turning her over. With extreme care, he removed the clamps. Then he moved her to the middle of the bed and lay beside her, pulling her against him. "Don't fight me," he instructed.

Surprising him, she obeyed. She laid her head on his biceps, and her hair spilled across him.

Outside, the sky's colour began to change as dusk cast shadows across the Rockies.

As she emerged from her place of pleasure-pain, he noticed subtle changes in her. Her breaths became deeper. Her body conformed to his. Her temperature stabilised. He kept hold of her, though, so she stayed warm.

"That was…"

He waited.

"One of the best beatings I've had."

One of the best? "I'll have to improve."

She scooted away so she could face him. "I meant it as a compliment, Sir."

He grinned and brushed hair back from her face. Her cheeks were still flushed. "Do you have bandages?"

"Mr Tomlinson?"

"This time, I fear my ego has sustained a mortal wound."

"Well, I'll volunteer my services so you can get more practise." She gave a long-suffering sigh.

Sexy and sassy. This was the Maggie he was beginning to know, buried beneath layers of professional clothes and a haughty demeanour. The more she revealed the real her, the deeper he wanted to excavate.

He pulled her tighter against him and held her while she dozed. When she awoke and looked up at him, he got a full-on erection.

"Your turn, I should say, Mr Tomlinson."

"Just to be clear, Maggie, I have no expectation that you have to sleep with me because I beat you."

"I was hoping you would."

He held her chin.

"It's part of it, for me," she admitted.

"I thought we had taken care of your restlessness."

"You did." Her big brown eyes were luminous. She blinked a couple of times, and if the woman was someone other than Maggie, he would have said the look was flirtatious. "Okay, fine," she said. "Is this what you want to hear? I'm horny."

He chuckled.

"I could give you a dozen emotional reasons, but I want sex. If you choose not to allow me to come, I accept that, but I really want your enormous, gigantic cock in me."

"'Enormous, gigantic cock'?" he couldn't help but repeat.

"I'm trying to repair the damage to your self-esteem, Mr Tomlinson. Shall I go on? Gorgeous dick. Perfect penis. Throbbing—"

"Where's that gag?"

"Are you going to do me, or what?"

"Well, when you ask so nicely..." He let her go long enough to get out of bed. He removed a condom from his wallet before placing it on the nightstand. Then he undressed and hung his clothes from a bedpost.

She turned on her side and propped her head on her upturned hand and watched as he put the condom on his dick.

"What *was* I thinking? That's a gargantuan cock," she said.

"Maggie... I think you're forgetting yourself."

She grinned and rolled to her back, spreading her legs in invitation. "Sorry, Mr Tomlinson."

"I'd give you a paddling, but you'd like it." He was as aroused as she was.

Maggie wrinkled her nose. "I could be brattier."

"In which case, I'll put you in a corner with your nose against the wall," he warned as he joined her on the bed.

Colour drained from her face. "I'll behave," she said.

"Maggie, you couldn't be any more wonderful."

He guided his cockhead towards her entrance. He intended to enter her with short strokes so that her body could accommodate him. "You weren't kidding about being horny."

"I'm wet for you, Sir."

He grabbed her hands and pinned them to the mattress above her.

"So hot," she told him.

They were good together. He slid inside her in a single surge.

"That's what I need. Hard, Mr Tomlinson." She bit her lower lip. "I mean, if that's all right?"

"I'll fuck you however you want it." He released his grip on her and said, "Put your legs around my waist." That forced her to lift her hips and gave him a different angle. "Keep some of your weight on your arms or elbows so you can keep yourself open for me." If she wanted a ride, he'd give it to her.

She looked at him, nothing but trust in her unblinking eyes.

It took all of his mental acuity not to lose himself in her hot cunt.

He drove into her again and again.

"This is... Damn. You're so deep in me."

Holding nothing back, he pounded her until she trembled, struggling to meet each of his surges. Her brow furrowed and she dug her heels into his back for purchase.

"Mr Tomlinson, I'm going to come," she said.

Her words were as much a question as a warning. "Do it," he instructed.

He felt her pussy clench and the constriction of her muscles milked his cock. He gritted his teeth, determined to satisfy her first.

He moved to put his hands beneath her buttocks, giving her extra support as she rode her orgasm.

She whimpered, and her body convulsed as she reached for it.

David spread her buttocks apart slightly and pressed his thumb into her anus.

Her scream rent the air.

Maggie broke position and grabbed his shoulders. She held onto him as she bucked and cried out.

For long seconds, she didn't breathe. Then he felt her internal pressure ease.

She ploughed her hand into his hair. "Thank you."

"Pleasuring you is an honour, Maggie."

"Now your turn," she said. "Before your big cock explodes."

He'd have glanced pointedly at the gag, but he didn't have the energy. If he were honest, he'd admit he didn't want to look away. All he wanted was to fuck her.

David removed his thumb and adjusted their positions a bit. "Put your buttocks on the mattress and grab the headboard." Once she did, he told her, "That's it." He had her where he wanted her, unable to move. He slid his hands beneath her and dug his fingers into the buttocks he'd reddened earlier.

With short, then lengthening strokes, he filled her. His orgasm built inside his balls. She muttered sounds of pleasure, feeding him.

"You fill me," she told him. "So, so full."

Knowing she was getting off was enough for him. It took less than thirty seconds for the orgasm to erupt from him — and that was what it felt like. It came from deep inside, hot and pulsing, joining them together.

He gritted his teeth as he filled the condom.

His nerve endings singed, he collapsed on her. God, this woman did it for him. Maybe it had been too long since he'd had sex with a woman he cared about. And perhaps it was the just effect of the curvy woman whose wild black hair matched her wanton abandon. Regardless, he hadn't had this sense of connection in a long time, if ever.

When he'd worked out on his rowing machine this morning, he hadn't anticipated the day ending like this. She wasn't the only one who would sleep well.

He disposed of the condom then returned to her and scooped her up. "We need a shower."

"We?"

"I'm not done with you yet. A shower will restore you for what I have in mind next."

Chapter Six

Last night, when David had said he had something in mind for her, he hadn't lied.

He'd washed her hair in the shower then lathered her body and inspected it for bruises. After they'd dried off, he'd asked if she had arnica. He'd massaged the white cream onto the marks then he'd rubbed down her entire body.

If this was his version of aftercare, she was sorry she'd missed out that night at the Den. She'd expected he might want to talk, but he hadn't. Instead, he'd put her on the side of the bed and fucked her from behind. He'd lasted a surprisingly long time, and he'd given her three orgasms before he'd claimed his own.

She'd fallen asleep in his arms, and it had been a long, long time since she'd done something like that.

Hours later, when her alarm had shattered the silence, he was gone. He hadn't left a note. Other than the residual tenderness in her body and the fact her clothes were still in the living room, there was no sign he'd been there at all.

As she grabbed a cup of coffee, it hit her.

She'd slept all night with no bad dreams.

Being with him had been everything she'd hoped. He'd given her the beating she wanted. She'd surrendered to it, to him. He'd been ruthless and persistent, sending her to subspace and keeping her there.

The way he'd brought her back had been sublime. He'd let her drift, but he'd kept her aware of his presence. She'd known that he was watching her. If she'd been in any distress, he would have taken care of it, with great competence, she was sure.

Maggie wondered if that was one of the problems she'd had with him when they'd first met. His confidence had irritated her. She'd wanted to label it as over-confidence, but over the past months, he'd backed up everything he'd said.

Now, rather than chafing under his control, she was accepting it. Last night, she'd flourished as a result.

Conscious of the time ticking away, she hurried through her shower then walked into her closet.

She recollected some of his comments from last night. He'd been verbal about her undergarments and that made her hesitate over what to choose. Every day, she wore stockings and a garter belt to work because she liked the feeling. Today, though, he'd know what was beneath her skirt.

Even if he didn't comment, their work dynamic would be altered.

She'd always been able to separate her BDSM scenes from the rest of her life, compartmentalising each piece. Of course, until now, she'd never had to face her Dom at the office the next day. Well, not that she'd ever had a true Dom before, either.

Maggie shuddered. She had been certain she could manage to work with him. After all, the contract wasn't forever and they didn't care about each other.

She snagged her lingerie for the day then shoved the drawer closed.

Before the scene had occurred, it had been easy to convince herself it was a good idea. Now the workday and reality loomed. Things appeared complicated.

In the mirror she saw a reflection of a red mark—a single welt—above the back of her knees. She fingered it the best she could with the awkward angle. Breath evaporated from her lungs. Even if she should, she didn't regret last night. In fact, she wanted more.

There it was. Honesty.

She wanted to see him again.

When he'd been selecting toys last night, he'd announced that they were spending the weekend together. Since the air between them had been charged with eroticism, she wasn't sure he'd meant it.

This was one of her biggest fears—the more BDSM scenes she got, the more she wanted.

With grim determination, keeping up a constant internal dialogue about how she could face him as if last night hadn't happened, she dressed.

For fortification, she added a blazer and took extra time with her hair.

She entered the offices feeling as if she were in control.

"The tyrant hasn't shown up yet," her mother said.

Agreeing with Gloria would feel disloyal to David.

"It's becoming a bad habit," Gloria continued.

"He was the first one here yesterday," Maggie said. She refused to add that she had no idea what time he'd made the drive from Littleton to Castle Rock.

Gloria had one elbow propped on the reception desk. A maxi skirt flowed over her hips and ended at her ankles. She wore thong sandals that showed off her toe rings and bright blue was splashed across her nails. Specks of white seemed dropped on the tops. She wondered if they were supposed to be flowers but couldn't be bothered asking.

Barb was leaning back in her chair, cup of coffee in one hand, as if enjoying the show.

"Is there more of that?" Maggie asked, pointing at the coffee.

"Knew you were coming in," Barb responded. "So it's extra strong." She made no attempt to go get a cup for Maggie.

Gloria's neon-green painted fingernails were in stark relief against her white drink.

"It's a tropical smoothie," Gloria explained without prompting. "Coconut water, pineapple juice, orange juice, with whey protein and an energy booster."

"Is that whipped cream on the top?"

"Non-dairy."

"Uh-huh," Maggie said.

"That's what I told the girl I wanted. Anyway, when the tyrant can be bothered to drag his carcass in for the day, I wanted to have a talk about the Tyler account."

"Isn't the meeting scheduled for ten o'clock?"

"No sense waiting."

"Which means you stayed up all night so you're already exhausted and want to go home?"

"Creative genius knows no bounds."

"Of course not." Maggie wondered how any left-brain activities had been done in the last few years. Had Gloria always been this eccentric? Or had David allowed her full artistic personality to blossom? Some might label her a nut, but she was turning out the best work Maggie had ever seen.

Their musings were interrupted when David walked through the door.

"Ladies."

Barb rolled her chair forwards and pretended to be working on the computer.

"*There* you are," Gloria said.

Did he have to look so freaking delicious? He wore a charcoal-grey suit with a crisp white shirt, accented by a conservative blue tie. No one looking at him right now would suspect he could swing his belt with such precision that he left almost no bruises behind. As she looked at him, she couldn't help but imagine him unknotting the tie and stuffing the silk in her mouth to muffle her screams. Until him, she hadn't fantasised about gags. But now that David had introduced her to one that he wore, she couldn't focus on anything else.

"Do I have something on me?"

She shook her head. "Sorry. I was lost in thought."

"Did you not sleep well?"

She met his gaze. The blue he wore made the colour of his eyes more startling than usual. Maggie felt heat creep up her neck to settle on her face. "I slept all the way through."

"Good to hear."

"If it's okay with you, can we cut the chit-chat and start the meeting early?" Gloria said.

"Am I allowed a cup of coffee first?"

Gloria made a dismissing signal with her free hand, jangling her requisite bracelets together.

"Twenty minutes?" David suggested. "As long as the conference room isn't booked?"

"It's free," Barb said after checking a calendar.

"Does that suit you, Maggie?"

"Me?" God, she wished that hadn't come out as a squeak rather than the cool question she had intended.

"You've got the final draft for approval, don't you, Gloria?"

She kept them waiting while she took a drink of her tropical, non-dairy whipped cream beverage. "I do."

"Good, then, Maggie, I do want you in the meeting." Briefcase in hand, he moved towards the break room.

"He's a hot man. I wonder if he works out. He has to, right?" Barb mused.

"He's a tyrant," Gloria said.

"I heard that," he said as he moved past them.

Humiliation crawled through Maggie, and she felt torn between loyalty to her boss and to her mother. "Keep it down next time," Maggie said. "Or better yet, strike it from your vocabulary."

"Whose side are you on—?"

"*You* are the artistic talent, Mother," Maggie said. "And he's giving you freedom to explore that."

"By having him look over my shoulder at every turn? Submitting my work for his approval? Checking up on me to be sure I got everything turned into his bookkeeper the moment I finish each step? It's suffocating." She broke the word into four distinct syllables.

"Then why are you producing more than you ever have before?" Maggie went in search of her own caffeine jolt.

When she returned to the reception area, Gloria was gone, but her waft of perfume was not. Barb grabbed an incoming phone call and avoided Maggie's gaze.

Maggie considered searching out David. But if this incident had happened before they'd slept together, she wouldn't have. If they were indeed keeping business and sex separate, she couldn't seek him out.

Besides, she had a pile of her own work to do, including finalising plans for the open house. A save-the-date email blast had gone out a while ago. Formal invitations were already in the mail. RSVPs had started to trickle in, and she and her mother would follow up with phone calls today.

It took only a few gulps to finish her coffee, and she refilled the cup on the way to the meeting.

David sought Maggie's opinion on the project then initialled his approval at the bottom of Gloria's work. "Nice job," he said.

"I'm going home to rest," Gloria said with a heavy, exaggerated sigh.

"You've earned it."

Leaving an aura of her drama behind, Gloria breezed from the room, leaving Maggie alone with David. He sat back and perused her, his attention making her body tingle.

She had a couple of things on her mind. First up was apologising for her mother's behaviour. Next came the assorted loose business ends she needed him to agree to. Most importantly, she was desperate to know if he was as affected by the previous evening as she was.

The moment she was about to break the silence, his cell phone rang. Excusing himself, he grabbed his belongings from the table and left the room as he answered his phone.

She collapsed against the chair, exhaling a breath she hadn't realised she'd been holding.

Determined to be as cool as he was—after all, she'd insisted they could be professional—she gathered her belongings then returned to her office. She sent David a couple of emails. He responded to one right away, the other took a couple of hours, frustrating her. She pounced on his incoming messages while he ignored hers?

When she left at the end of the day, his office door was closed.

The next morning, she found a piece of paper on her desk. His bold scrawl filled the page. He'd given her his home address and added that he expected to see her mid-afternoon on Saturday.

She gripped the note. From anyone else, she might find the instructions and assumptions off-putting. For her, this was like much-needed oxygen. For the first time since he'd left her condo, she relaxed.

Later in the day, they met in the privacy of his office to discuss the potential merger and for her to solicit his input on the first drafts of the logo for the combined companies. He approved the picture of the eagle but said he was not pleased with the font selected for the company name. She agreed with his revisions then brought him up-to-date on plans for the open house.

When they'd exhausted their agenda items, she waited a moment to see if he had anything to add. Since he didn't mention their upcoming weekend, she didn't bring it up.

* * * *

The remainder of the week dragged, each minute seeming like two. Maggie was excited and edgy like she was before her trips to the Den. She'd ordered new shoes and couldn't wait to wear them for him.

She filled Saturday morning with a trip to the gym, doing laundry then cleaning. She even took a trip to the grocery store for the following week. With any luck, she wouldn't be home until late Sunday.

David hadn't given any instructions on what she should wear, so she chose a shelf bra to leave her nipples exposed, knowing he'd accept the unspoken invitation to touch. She added a matching garter belt and fishnet stockings before slipping into a short skirt and figure-hugging shirt. She finished off with new, hot-as-sin, spiky heels and hoped she didn't regret the selection. If the terrain around his house was uneven, she might end up sprawled at his feet.

When she neared his home, her phone beeped, signalling an incoming text message.

He'd sent her a single word.

Soon.

Her speedometer read ten miles an hour over the posted limit. Getting stopped by a police officer while dressed like this wasn't on her to-do list.

She eased off the accelerator, cranked up an oldies song on the satellite radio and sang along. She couldn't carry a tune, but the noise drowned out the nervous thoughts skittering through her mind.

After she left the highway, she turned down the radio so she could follow the instructions from her GPS. She meandered west for several miles. Houses became farther apart and civilisation seemed to disappear.

She left the main road and still had to drive a few miles to reach his place.

Though she'd lived in Colorado almost her entire life, she'd had no idea that these houses on acres of verdant, rolling land existed.

As the GPS showed she was nearing her destination, her pulse picked up. She was cognisant of her exposed nipples and the sensitive way they felt against the fabric of her shirt. She and David had been together twice before, and she told herself she should be nonchalant about their upcoming night together. She was anything but.

Thoughts crowded into her mind, jostling for position.

She'd slept badly again last night, and had tossed the bedding off her perspiration-drenched body. She'd climbed out of bed, had a glass of water and waited for the nightmares to recede. What had replaced them was scarier — the realisation that David held the key to keeping the bad dreams at bay.

Maggie turned the car into his driveway and braked to a stop on the steep concrete. The setting was idyllic, remote and quiet, a contrast to the high-density area where she lived. Out here she heard birds, including the screech of a red-tailed hawk.

Hands shaking from the sudden onslaught of excitement, she killed the engine and reached for the bag she'd placed on the passenger seat.

She exited the vehicle to see David standing in the entryway with the door open. His left shoulder was braced on the doorjamb, his feet were crossed. He held a glass of something that might be white wine.

The bright sunshine danced on his dark hair. Damp ends clung to his nape.

She'd seen him dressed for business both in suits and in jeans with an armband when he'd been serving as House Monitor. Whether he was bare-chested or had rolled back his shirtsleeves and exposed his forearms before he beat her, the sight of him stimulated her.

Here on his own turf, he seemed somehow even more competent and in control. The Den was Master Damien's territory. At her condominium, she felt comfortable. This sprawling house and grounds was his domain. He didn't own it, he dominated it.

Maggie knew she hadn't made a mistake coming here, and the butterflies battering around in her tummy were more thrilling than upsetting. She wanted everything he had in store for her.

He moved towards her as she slammed the car door shut.

His black T-shirt conformed to his muscular frame. Blue jeans rode low on his hips. He'd skipped a belt, but his motorcycle boots added a rakish air.

David Tomlinson made her mouth water.

"Welcome," he said, his voice thick and foreboding. He took her bag and indicated she should precede him inside.

The massive, sun-drenched foyer took her breath. Arched windows soared two storeys. She hadn't expected his place to be such an interesting mix of modern and eclectic. Metal and wood. And stunningly, a waterfall flowed down the far living room wall. Sectional furniture had been positioned to take in the ambiance, and she could imagine sitting there, lost in creative thought. "I might never leave."

"Good plan."

Their gazes met.

She'd said her words with flippant disregard, like she did when she vacationed at a fancy resort. But he'd responded with a seriousness that resonated deep inside her.

For a moment, she considered what it might be like to have him come home to her and the expectations that went with that. She wasn't sure she could manage it.

He placed her bag at the bottom of the stairs. "How about a glass of wine? We'll have dinner a bit later.

Steak and salad? You'll need to keep your energy up for what I have in mind."

"I..." The reminder that they would be spending the night together chilled her. "Yes. To both. Thanks."

"Let me show you around so you feel comfortable. If you need anything, ask for it or help yourself. I don't stand on ceremony."

She followed him into the kitchen.

A bottle of wine stood on the stone-topped island with a glass next to it. The appliances were top of the line.

"Hot tub outside," he said as he poured a glass. "I'll put you in it before bed to loosen your muscles."

"I didn't bring a swimsuit."

"You wouldn't be allowed to wear it even if you had."

When they were together, he exerted his dominance in dozens of subtle, thrilling ways.

"Join me?"

She accepted the glass of wine and took a sip while he opened the French doors and walked onto the deck. Maggie was careful with her shoes so she didn't get her heels jammed between the redwood boards.

"Naked is better," he said.

"What about splinters?"

"I have the wood refinished every year. Believe me, Maggie, your safety is of utmost importance."

The tub was in its own gazebo off to the right of the deck. There were numerous built- in benches and a couple of different tables placed near them. The southern portion of the area was shaded by a trellis covered with vines, and other areas were exposed to soak up the sun. "Is this where you have your morning coffee?"

"Even when I have to shovel off the snow. The colder it is, the better the hot tub feels."

There was a manicured area then the wilderness claimed the property.

"Is that a deer out there?"

"Very likely."

She followed him back inside. "I love the living room."

"We'll begin our play there."

He picked up her bag and carried it up the stairs. A loft overlooked the first floor. He had a home office, all black and chrome with a glass desk. Two enormous flat-screen monitors formed a straight line. That left little space for personal effects.

"This looks like command central." *Only more sterile.*

"I spend most of my time here," he said.

He needed someone to jazz up his life.

After showing her a couple of guest bedrooms, he led her to the master bedroom. A bed dominated the space, and it had a slatted headboard. That sent chills of possibility racing through her system.

David placed her bag in an empty closet.

"This is yours to use. Feel free to leave anything you'd like. Not that I've forgotten that I want to go through your toy box and all your lingerie as well."

His words hinted at something more serious than she'd been anticipating. Since she didn't know how to respond, she remained silent.

She peeked inside the bathroom and didn't see a bathtub, not that he needed one. The massive shower unit had no door. Outside of designer magazines, she'd never seen anything like it.

"I want you to feel comfortable here, Maggie."

"In that case, I may take several showers a day."

"I understand the temptation." He grinned. "I'll be downstairs. Feel free to clean up, if you wish. Towels are in the drawers beneath the vanity. I'll see you in the living room when you're ready." At the door, he paused and looked back at her. "Be naked."

He left, and she heard his footfall on the open, wooden stairs.

She collapsed against the wall. So much for all the time and care she had taken with her clothes.

Mindful he was waiting, she channelled her concentration into getting ready for him. She took a sip of the dry white wine. She was sure the vintage was excellent, but she put it down after one sip, too nervous to drink much of it. After pulling off her shoes, she entered the closet—her closet—to remove everything else. Not only had he provided an assortment of hangers, but there was a built-in chest of drawers.

Now that she was naked, she couldn't resist showering. She grabbed an oversized towel from one of the drawers. With the way they were so precisely folded and stacked, she wondered if he had a housekeeper. If not, he was more fastidious than she'd believed.

The waterfall shower invigorated her. Since she'd drained the hot water tank, she hoped he had no plans beyond a cold shower, if he needed one.

Her heart hammered as she descended the staircase, her hand curved around the chrome banister.

She heard the sounds of splashing water as she neared the living room. Chilled air whispered across her skin, pebbling her nipples. At least that's what she told herself—it might have been the anticipation churning in her that caused the reaction.

He was on the couch, one arm across the back, a fresh glass of wine in the other. "Stand there," he said, pointing.

An overhead skylight lit the hardwood floor, and she welcomed the warmth.

"As sexy as your clothes are, I like to see all of you. It's tempting to keep you here, nude and chained for my pleasure."

She looked at him, unable to ascertain whether or not he was joking.

He slid his drink onto the square coffee table and picked up a pair of clamps. She frowned. She'd been honest that she started with a light weight and worked her way up, but it didn't appear she would feel these little pieces of plastic at all. Boring.

"Put your hands behind your head and spread your legs as far apart as you can without causing cramps."

She got into position, aware of him watching her. He stood and walked towards her. He reached between her legs and played with her pussy.

In response, she angled her pelvis towards him, offering more and hoping for an orgasm.

Shocking her, he tugged on her labia and attached the clamps. "*God.*"

"My thoughts exactly," he said, stepping back.

No way would they have aroused her nipples, but on her most tender flesh, they burned.

"Bend over and grab your ankles. I want to inspect your body."

Knowing better than to argue with a Dom, she followed his instructions.

He moved behind her. "You have one small bruise above your knee. How are your arms?"

"Unblemished."

"You sound disappointed."

"I am."

"You want to show up for work on Monday with a few bruises to remember me by?"

She was glad her hair curtained her face so she couldn't see him. It emboldened her. "Yes."

"Since you don't bruise easily, I'm not as concerned about playing for an extended period of time," he said.

"As long as you think you are capable of handling me all by yourself, Mr Tomlinson." She knew she was skating close to the line between teasing and disrespect. Part of her didn't want to cross it, but the naughty part of her, the one hurt by his actions, urged her to be reckless. As much as she hated to admit it, the fact he'd all but ignored her since their scene at her condo had irritated her. There was no reason he couldn't have contacted her after work hours.

"I think I'm up for the challenge." He tugged on her clamps.

Yelping, she released her ankles briefly then, realising what she had done, grabbed them again.

"Do you have something to say, Maggie?"

Was he a mind reader all of a sudden? "No, Sir."

"You know, little submissive, you can ask for what you want. I was serious the other day when I told you I'd put you in a corner with your nose against the wall for your misbehaviour."

As it had before, the threat frightened her. She'd never been one for timeouts. Being separated from those she cared about while they went on with their lives was emotionally debilitating. "I... I apologise, Mr Tomlinson."

"Just so we're clear, that will be my discipline of choice. I don't think a punishment spanking would work with you."

She shivered.

"Maggie?"

"I think it might be more effective than you realise. Anything that has caused your anger would upset me." She struggled for words. "It's different."

"Agreed. But you'd have a mark to remember it, and you might get off on that."

How well he knew her.

"I will never touch you in anger or until we've had the chance to speak. I urge you to talk to me about anything that bothers you. Come to me, Maggie. Trust me. We can work through anything as long as we do it together."

She was starting to get dizzy from being upside down. Her pussy pulsed from the clamps and, even though they were together, she felt distant.

"Tell me you understand."

"I do, Mr Tomlinson."

"Save yourself from my wrath by hiding nothing from me."

"You're asking a lot."

"No more than what I'm willing to give." He kept her there for another few minutes in silence, likely giving her a chance to reflect on his words, before he relented. "You may stand."

Once she had done and had placed her hands behind her head, he said, "I'll repeat myself. Since your comment was out of line, is there anything you need to discuss?"

"I…"

He sat on the couch, glass of wine once again in hand.

"I thought I wanted to pretend we'd never been together. It's harder than I'd imagined."

"Even when your mother and the staff have nothing kind to say about me?"

Her blood froze. "Are you angry with me?" If so, why had he invited her here?

"Not at all. I wouldn't agree to scene with you if I was angry. You deserve only a scene in which the Dom is calm. I'm disappointed. I had hoped the staff would have learnt we're on the same team."

Even though the criticism wasn't aimed at her, it stung, mostly because he made an excellent point. She had defended him, but she should have been doing that from the beginning rather than participating in the gossip. "Is that why you've avoided me all week?"

"Is that what's bothering you?" he countered.

"Yes." She exhaled. "I missed you."

"Fuck." He leant forwards and placed the glass of wine on the table top. "Maggie, if you think this is easier for me than it is you, you're wrong. You were the one who came to my office and laid down the expectations before that scene. I was trying to abide by your wishes when what I wanted to do was bend you over and spank you for wearing stockings and a garter belt to work."

His admission comforted her in a way she hadn't expected. "I didn't sleep well last night," she admitted.

"You will tonight."

Again, that confidence, assuredness, arrogance. He undid her.

"How difficult was it to unburden yourself?"

"Not as bad as I feared," she confessed.

"Remember this. Turn to me, not from me."

"Again, Sir, you have no idea what you're asking of me." She hadn't had anyone to look after her before, and had never had a sexual relationship where she felt free to unburden herself.

"A few turns in the corner might add some incentive."

Maggie shivered.

"Sub's choice. If we're going to do this on a regular basis, I demand your honesty. If you cannot offer it, I can't trust you. If you don't like my rules, you can safe word out and leave at any time."

"Ah…"

"Question?"

"If I use my safe word, I have to leave?"

"God, no. I'm just saying you have the ultimate power. I have none beyond what you give me. Understand?"

The ease with which he'd discerned something was wrong then uncovered it should have upset her. Instead, it liberated her. She'd never known anyone who cared enough to even try. All the other men, whether in a scene or a vanilla relationship, had allowed her to hide. He was unnerving.

"I need you to touch me." The clamps now burned as much as his physical distance chafed.

"Nothing would please me more." He moved his drink to the floor and slid it against the couch for protection. Then he opened the top of the coffee table.

An array of spanking implements rested on black velvet. "That's a clever toy box, Mr Tomlinson."

"Another of Master Marcus' functional designs. He seems inspired these days."

"I'd say." Who needed a dungeon when you could keep all your naughty secrets hidden in plain sight?

He looked at her.

"This was why you checked me for bruises," she said.

"You're onto my nefarious plan. I planned to make my selection with care."

Despite the tension, she smiled. He returned it. The shared moment made the world seem as if it were back on its axis.

He chose a tawse.

"That's serious, Sir."

"Any objection?"

She licked her dry lips. Thrill and trepidation churned a potent mixture in her stomach. "Hell no."

"I didn't think there would be." After closing the lid, he instructed, "Over my lap."

"Yes, Mr Tomlinson."

"Crawl to me."

That wasn't something she'd ever been instructed to do. She'd never understood the appeal. But once she had lowered herself to all fours, comprehension dawned. Being on the floor changed her perspective, making her mindful of her submissiveness. Her body moved in a different way. Her breasts hung low, her hips swayed and the addition of the clamps exposed her pussy.

"I like having you naked and on your knees," he said. "That's how I'll keep you."

When she looked up and saw the approval in his electric blue eyes, she was convinced he meant what he said. The way he perused her made her insides melt.

She draped herself over his knee, and he jostled her so that her ass was high.

"As you know, this will be worse than the flogger or my hand and likely worse than my belt. There's no shame in needing a break or requesting something else."

"I understand."

"You may hold onto my leg if you need to."

The wait seemed interminable.

She'd hoped he'd get on with it, but he rubbed and teased her before applying the rigid leather thong to her skin.

The first stroke across her butt stole her breath.

She'd only experienced a tawse once before, and it had never been as debilitating as this.

The pain screamed through her body and she knew it had left a scorching mark across her skin. The clamps were uncomfortable, intensifying the sensation.

He paused, and she took a breath to compose herself.

"When you're ready, put your ass back up in the air."

"Yes, Mr Tomlinson," she said. It took her another few seconds to comply.

He was ruthless and methodical. There was nothing random about the way he moved lower with each stroke. Knowing what to expect didn't make it easier to take. He paused between each hit, and she was grateful for the respite, something she'd never before needed during a spanking.

She screamed when he caught the backs of her knees.

"Gorgeous colour of red," he told her.

For a moment, she considered using her slow word, but the immediacy of the pain faded, leaving behind the familiar and welcomed sense of satisfaction.

"On your toes, sub," he instructed. "Turn your toes in a little so I have better access."

Earlier this week, from the soothing rhythm of his belt, she'd reached subspace. She wouldn't get there this time, she knew. This was beyond anything she'd experienced.

"Maggie," he prompted.

"Sir…" Thoughts were more difficult to string together than they ever had been.

"Do you need me to repeat myself?"

His voice didn't vibrate with hostility, instead he was calm, probing. With great concentration, she recalled his instruction. She dug the balls of her feet into the floor beneath her and used the leverage to rise up and spread her legs.

"Can you endure another ten?"

She wasn't sure. No doubt she could have if she didn't know how many were coming. But ten? After what she had already been through? At this point, she wasn't sure where her limit was.

"For me," he said.

If she looked at him with his chiselled, stern cheekbones, she would be lost. With her eyes closed, she considered her decision.

"You can set the pace by how quickly you get back into position."

She was learning she could deny this man nothing. "Give me your best, Mr Tomlinson." Even she heard the bravado in her statement.

"You're brave, Maggie."

He blazed the first one on her right thigh. She lowered herself as she waited for the agony to recede. He hadn't caught both thighs and diminished the impact. Instead, he'd intensified it.

Gritting her teeth, she signalled she was ready for the next.

"It's okay to cry," he told her as he laid into her again.

"No way, Sir," she responded. She meant it. At this point, it was a matter of pride.

The third and fourth hits from the stern implement almost destroyed her resolve. He'd told her she could hold onto his leg, so she did. It was more a death grip than for balance.

He was deliberate with his placement, delivering more pain than she'd ever experienced. She'd heard there was a specific way to use a tawse, and he'd mastered it.

"Almost there," he said. "Three more."

The relentless assault continued, each swat jarring the clamps and making her pussy sore.

"Last one," he told her.

Since she couldn't move, he positioned her ass where he wanted it.

"That's it."

The crack across her ass reverberated through the room, joined by her scream.

He tossed the tawse on the coffee table and gathered her close to him.

She turned her cheek against him, into him and sought refuge in his solid muscles and the softness of his cotton shirt.

Tears she refused to release stung her eyes, and she blinked them back. She trembled and shook, and he held her.

The spanking had humbled her.

Until him, she had refused aftercare. But the other night at her condo, she'd surrendered to it. Being vulnerable in those first few minutes after such an intense experience had made the experience richer. She didn't have to savour it alone like she had always done.

By measures, she noticed the rich rumble of his voice even if she couldn't understand his words. Finally, something about removing her clamps penetrated her haze. "Yes, please."

"Spread your legs."

"My body feels as if it's rubber," she admitted.

He helped her to move, and she was nervous to have the clamps removed. Without any fuss, he removed them and dropped the mean little pieces alongside the tawse. That would teach her to underestimate him again.

"I think you've earned an orgasm."

He laid her down and raised her legs over his shoulders. He placed a pillow under her hips then licked her cunt.

"Mr Tomlinson!"

He pinched her labia where the clamps had been affixed. The flesh was tender and his touch drove her mad. She whimpered and squirmed, but he wouldn't be deterred.

The leather couch beneath her raw legs and buttocks magnified the agony.

He finger fucked her, licked her, sucked her, pinched her and, when she couldn't take any more, slid a finger up her tightest hole.

She shattered from the inside out, coming with a hoarse cry as she shamelessly lifted her hips and begged for more.

He obliged, plunging his tongue in her hot moistness then licking her clit.

"I'm going to come again," she warned him.

He increased his motions and brought her off, leaving her feeling as if she had nothing more to give.

"Let's get you in the shower so I can see to your bruises."

Her whole body was sensitised. Her pussy throbbed. The back of her legs and buttocks still felt aflame from his tawse.

His attention to her body wasn't the worst of it. The way he read her desires — then met them — had pushed her beyond where she'd ever gone before. She hadn't known she could take that much pain.

What he demanded from her emotionally was something else — he allowed her no secrets. He'd sensed there was something wrong with her when she fired off a smartass reply earlier. His ability to see her upset and hurt disturbed her.

She'd never met anyone like him, and she knew the experience would change her. She hoped she'd survive it.

He scooped her from the couch.

"You can't do this," she protested, grabbing on tightly.

"Because?"

"I'm too heavy."

He looked at her. "I want you to be clear on this, Maggie, I've got you. In all ways."

The reassurance frightened her more than anything.

Upstairs, he deposited her on the bed while he turned on the shower. When he returned for her, he was naked. His cock was glorious in its arousal. She wanted it in her with a desperation she'd never had before. "I am certain I can walk on my own," she told him.

"I think you'll do as you're told."

He carried her into the shower and detached the showerhead to cool off her body. Afterwards, he wrapped her in a towel then carried her back to the bedroom where he rubbed arnica into her reddened spots.

"You may have one or two bruises."

"From the way it felt, I expected more than that."

"The weekend is young," he said.

He pulled on a pair of thin workout pants, a clean T-shirt and sandals.

"You won't need clothing," he told her as she headed for her closet. "I'll adjust the temperature so you're comfortable."

"That seems...awkward."

"Natural," he challenged. "And it's how a Dom behaves," he said, his feet shoulder-width apart and his arms folded across his chest. "You can fight me all you want, but I will win."

She scowled at him. Hanging out in the nude seemed different to her than when they were sceneing.

"Stay there." He went into his closet and came back with a strip of lilac-coloured leather.

"What's that?" she asked unnecessarily.

"A reinforcement of your role," he told her. "It means what we say it does, nothing more."

"And to you?"

"It will keep you in the right frame of mind."

"The naked kind."

He inclined his head. They were having a disagreement, and they both seemed to know it.

"You can take it off at any time and put your clothing back on."

David had softened his tone, and she responded to that.

She'd donned a collar for her night at the Den. That had been for kicks, nothing more. It amazed her how much more laden this felt.

"Kneel."

Her temptation was to rebel, but she realised they were fighting over scraps of fabric. She'd packed little more than lingerie and some don't-appear-in-public skirts. He'd have the same access to her body regardless.

"Tell me the problem."

"I'll have no way to hide," she admitted to both of them.

"That's why I want you nude."

At times she wasn't sure she liked him much.

"Now kneel, Maggie."

Something primitive, as old as the heartbeat of time, responded to his dominance.

Looking up at him, she obeyed. Her face was near his crotch, and the masculine scent of him combined with the power of his body to make her feel utterly feminine.

"Mine," he said as he buckled the collar closed.

She was scared that was true, and more frightened that it might not be.

Chapter Seven

"Have a seat," David told Maggie, indicating a stool beneath the stone countertop.

She did as he'd instructed—her motions deliberate.

"Trying to get comfortable should be impossible. If it's not, I can give you a second beating now."

"I'm fine," she said, her words a jumbled rush. "Thank you, Mr Tomlinson."

"More wine?"

"Please."

From the living room, he collected his unfinished glass.

"Mine's upstairs, I'm afraid."

"I'll get it later." He put his in the dishwasher then asked, "Red to go with the steak?"

"I'll stick with the white unless it offends your sensibilities."

"You should have whatever you prefer, and don't let anyone tell you otherwise." He uncorked a bottle of red and poured her a white. He liked having her collared, naked body in his kitchen. Other than when he'd hosted a party for several people, he'd never invited a woman to his house.

Since his divorce from Sandy, he hadn't had the inclination to share his space. But with this dark-haired beauty, he hadn't had a choice. The other night, he'd realised a few hours wouldn't satiate his need for her.

All week, he'd noticed her growing frustration when he'd stayed away from her at work. But he'd needed some time to think things through. What the hell was he supposed to do when he knew he wanted uninterrupted time together, but was honest enough to admit he was a less than perfect partner when it came to committed relationships? He hadn't just failed with Sandra—he'd been guilty of withholding attention no matter who his partner was, be she submissive or vanilla.

He'd known that spending more time with Maggie would take a concerted effort on his part. He hadn't been sure he was capable of expending the energy on a long-term basis, or if she'd appreciate it even if he did. She'd been clear that sceneing was all she wanted. Once he'd reached his decision, about twenty minutes into a run on Wednesday morning, he'd set his sights on having her. He'd turned part of his considerable energies towards figuring out how to make it happen.

He'd wanted her as hungry for him as he was for her.

He'd wanted privacy and a place where she was out of her element. His house. With no clothes.

Objective accomplished. Not that he'd doubted it would happen. They wanted each other bad enough to break all their self-imposed rules.

For the first time that he could remember, he'd left work early on Friday night. As he'd blazed through the grocery store with at least two hundred other people then cruised the aisles at the supersized liquor store, he'd realised that he'd never made the time for a relationship. Wanting to be available for all her needs, he'd climbed out of bed at five a.m. to exercise, answer emails and plan next week's schedule before Maggie arrived.

It was hard for him to admit he'd been a jerk before. Not that it should have come as a surprise. He'd been told that often enough.

He slid Maggie's drink towards her.

She glanced around before taking a sip.

"You can relax. It's just us."

He noticed she crossed her legs then uncrossed them again and pulled back her shoulders. Within seconds, she'd curled back into herself.

"Stand up," he told her, the words clipped and commanding.

"Sir?"

"You heard me."

She released her glass and followed his command.

"Bend over the stool."

Her eyes widened.

He moved towards her and fisted her hair. "Now." He waited a moment for her to safe word before forcing her down.

Her muskiness flooded his senses. The woman might fight him, but she was turned on.

This wasn't meant as a punishment, more it was a reinforcement of their roles and a physical way to jar her out of her discomfort. "Count them," he instructed as she grasped the stool's legs for balance. He gave her the first spank with his open hand on her right buttock. "I said count," he snapped when she remained silent. This was a battle of wills, and he wouldn't lose.

"One, Mr Tomlinson."

He gave her four more slaps in quick succession, forcing gasps out of her. Earlier he'd let her be in charge of the pace if not the number. This time, he took even that from her.

"Three, four, five, Mr Tomlinson."

He moved to the other butt cheek.

She gasped and cried out, carrying on instead of counting. He wanted her tears, wanted to break through her resolve.

When her chest was heaving and her body blazed with his marks, he helped her to stand. He kept a firm grip on her shoulders as he said, "Thank me."

"Thank you, Mr Tomlinson," she whispered.

He liked her compliance. "You were right that you need spankings. Regular ones. Now that I know that, I'll be sure you always have one. I'll keep a belt or hairbrush handy. Back on your stool." He helped her, and she trembled, keeping her gaze down.

Giving her a quick thrashing shouldn't turn him on as much as it did. He told himself he should be able to deliver it dispassionately. Good Doms were capable of separating their corrective actions from their arousal.

There were moments with her, though, when that didn't seem possible. Forcing her out of her self-conscious prison meant he had to rein in his libido. He released her and put the distance of the kitchen between them. He took the steaks out of the refrigerator and brushed on his homemade sauce before setting them aside to marinate. He poured his wine and swirled it in the glass before levelling his gaze on her. "Masturbate."

"I... *What?*"

"Get yourself off. Don't tell me you can't. I know you're aroused from my spanking as well as my dominance. Do it."

To her credit, she didn't look around. She kept her gaze on him, even if she did hesitate.

"My request is not negotiable," he said.

She worried her upper lip.

Hard to believe this was the same woman who challenged him at every turn in the office. "Would you like me to put your labia clamps back on as punishment?"

"No thank you, Sir. I'm good."

"Then get on with it." He leant back against the counter while she parted her pussy lips. "I want to hear you. Be verbal."

Once she got past this, being spanked and playing with herself in the kitchen, she'd feel no more embarrassment.

She moistened a finger and slid it across her clit. Still watching him, she repeated the move several times.

"That's hot," he said.

After a few more strokes, she closed her eyes. As he'd wanted, she expressed herself in whimpers and moans.

"Do you like that, Maggie?"

"Oh, definitely, Mr Tomlinson. My clit is pounding and it feels…" She tipped her head back. *"Damn.* So, so good. I'm pretending it's you touching me."

His cock hardened. Who was being punished here?

He shoved away the wine and went to find his wallet. Where in the hell had he left it? He found it on a table near the front door. Trying for the control he was nowhere close to harnessing, he dug out a condom. Cash spilled out and he didn't care. His mind was filled with one thing — Maggie. "Such a good sub," he told her when he returned to the kitchen to find her still toying with her cunt. "I have to have you now." He shucked his sandals and pants then donned the sheath.

"Mr Tomlinson…"

None of this had been his intention. He'd planned a nice dinner, conversation in the living room then a long, deep fuck in bed. But the sight of her in a collar—permanent or not—as she pleasured herself was too much for any mere mortal man.

He removed her from the stool and bent her over it. Their height difference was a slight challenge. "Feet together and stand on your toes." He knew that would make the fit even tighter, and he relished it.

David spread his legs wide and parted her buttocks with his palms.

"Sir is so hot," she murmured.

"Sub is slick." He surged up into her welcoming heat. Once he was balls-deep, he reached around to fondle her nipples.

"I'm not going to last long, Mr Tomlinson." She constricted her muscles hard enough that he slid out of her.

"You are so fucking responsive, Maggie. I'm going to keep you cuffed to my bed."

"Promises, promises," she retorted.

He repositioned himself so he could slip back inside her. Consumed by heat and lust, he rocked his pelvis. His engorged cock throbbed with demand. He thrust and she gasped, urging him on.

This woman matched his sexual desire and clouded his brain. Nothing with her went as he thought it would. Possession was the only thing on his mind.

She milked the ejaculate from his cock in less time than it had taken him to come as a teenager.

Replete, breathless, he eased out of her then turned her to face him. He feathered back hair from her face. Then he did something that would have been uncharacteristic with any other submissive. He kissed her. The gentle brush was insufficient. Holding her imprisoned, he licked across her lower lip then said, "Open for me."

She was softness and surrender as she leaned into him, wrapping her arms around his neck.

He tasted the white wine. With his mouth and hands on her, he tried to convey the feelings he couldn't otherwise express. She was different from any woman he'd ever had. She challenged him, she pissed him off. And he would claim her.

She met his tongue parry for parry. Then she deepened the kiss, driving into his mouth. While he'd intended to be the one to send a message, she was the one who succeeded. She'd submit to him because she chose to, and never because he demanded it.

That made him respect her even more.

Maggie was so right for him.

With great reluctance, knowing they both needed to breathe and he had to discard the condom, he dragged himself away from her.

"Well, wow, Mr Tomlinson."

"I couldn't have said it better myself." He grabbed up his pants and said, "Be right with you."

When he returned, she had settled herself on the stool again. Her shoulders were back, giving him a beautiful view of her breasts and erect nipples. Her hair flowed over her shoulders and she held a wineglass, appearing at ease.

"Sex and a submissive mindset seem to agree with you."

She lowered her gaze to the countertop.

"Don't be ashamed of that. It pleases me more than you know." He topped off her glass.

"I could get accustomed to being spoilt like this."

"So you should. I suspect you've been solving the world's problems for a few years."

"My own, at least. My dad passed when I was young."

"And you took care of yourself." It wasn't a question. He'd seen the way she interacted with Gloria. The other woman was brilliant in her way, but he suspected she'd been hands-off as a parent. In fact, Maggie seemed more nurturing than her mother was.

"It wasn't all bad," Maggie said. "I learnt how to be independent and think for myself."

He prepared the salad then tossed the steaks on the grill to a rewarding hiss and sizzle.

"Can I help set the table?" she asked when he came back inside.

"Plates are there." He pointed to a cupboard. "Silverware is over there. Placemats and napkins are in that drawer."

"Fancy."

"We'll be dining al fresco."

She opened her mouth.

"Save your breath for an argument you can win," he urged. "The weather is beautiful and the deck is private. No one will see you."

She closed her mouth again. Mutely she worked around him, gathering items and making a few trips outside.

"If you weren't so stubborn, we could enjoy working together," he said.

"You're the one who makes the rules wherever we are, Mr Tomlinson."

"You could be a bit more agreeable when you follow them."

"Am I the only one who has to bend, Sir?" she asked as she walked past him.

The words walloped him. No doubt he liked to have things his way, always had. But, in addition to his other faults, was he that inflexible?

He grabbed a platter for the steaks then went outside. A water glass sat on the top of the table, filled with flowers from his garden. In that moment he realised how sterile his home was. Since Sandy had insisted everything in their old house have sentimental meaning, he'd let her keep all of it. When he'd bought this house, he'd hired a designer to furnish it. The only thing he'd had any input on had been the bed. He missed the touches a woman could provide. "Table looks great. Thank you for the help," he said.

She sipped from her glass.

"How do you want your steak?"

"Medium-rare. Unless it's already too late?"

"Should be perfect." He served them both, and it seemed she relaxed — he liked the transformation.

"Delicious," she told him after taking a bite. "Like you said, I need my strength."

"You have no idea."

The more comfortable she became, the sexier her movements were. Though he'd just fucked her, he couldn't wait to have her again.

"You know, Maggie, your slow word is for use any time."

"Mr Tomlinson?" she asked, putting down her utensils.

"Inside, when you asked if you were the only one who has to bend... I'm not sure if you were trying to express your displeasure at me telling you that we were going to eat outside, or whether you meant something more serious by it that you need to discuss. I understand you think I'm being somewhat high-handed, and the truth is, you're right."

"Well then," she said. "That settles that."

"I'm a Dom, Maggie. You're a sub."

"So you know what's best for me?"

"Maybe not," he admitted. "But I do know I love looking at you. I spent far too much time this morning picturing your naked body in the sunshine."

"Damn it, Mr Tomlinson."

"It's not just about bending you to my will — "

"Though that's an added bonus," she interrupted.

"Agreed. But it's about appreciating you and your willingness to do things to please me." He gave her a chance to respond. "Speechless?" he asked into the silence.

"I'm not very good at putting your needs first, I suppose."

"Hence the constant battle. At work, Maggie, my track record shows I do know what's best for the bottom line. Even there, I don't act without consulting you. I wonder if you're fighting me for the sake of fighting me, for what you feel is your independence. We've proved time and again that we work well together." He paused. "When you let us."

She sat back.

"Tell me, Maggie, when have I demanded something irrational? You have to admit the company is better for your involvement."

"The company, yes."

"And how have I stifled your earning potential or creativity or authority?"

"You haven't." She reached for her empty wineglass and rolled the stem between her palms. "Having you in charge has been an adjustment."

"You were under no duress when you came here," he reminded her.

"I think..." She stared into her glass for at least thirty seconds before looking up at him with her guileless brown eyes. "To you, it's not just about the spanking and getting me off, is it?"

"Not even close," he said, voice flat. "I will do everything in my power to please you and give you multiple orgasms, but I expect reciprocity. I don't mean in terms of sex, I mean respect." Though he'd made an attempt to be flexible, he realised he'd again sounded dictatorial. "Look, Maggie, I'm screwing this up."

"No. You're not. I get it. You're right. I have been accusing you of being an ogre, and I've been worse. You're right that we collaborate well. And it's unfair of me to be compliant when we're being sexual but then refuse to cooperate in other ways." She leant forwards. "I apologise, Mr Tomlinson."

"I'll bend, Maggie. Or at least I'll try. Use a slow word if I don't. Communicate with me. I need you to meet me halfway. Don't make me guess what's wrong when you have an issue with something I've requested."

"That's a tall order, Sir."

"You told me earlier you've been on your own for years. You can do this."

She sighed. "You're right, Mr Tomlinson."

They cleared the table together. She loaded the dishwasher while he put away the leftover salad.

"How are you feeling?" he asked her afterwards.

"A bit uncertain." She wrapped her arms around her middle. "We scened, fucked, ate."

"Are you afraid I'll make you snuggle up and watch racing or something like that on television?"

She laughed.

"I've got plenty more in store for you. You haven't seen the basement yet."

Her eyes widened.

"Open that door," he told her. "And go on down. I'll join you in a minute." He grabbed a couple of bottles of water, wanting her to have time to explore the area on her own.

The area was finished, and it was large. He'd had the pool table removed and had taken out several walls for his exercise space. While he'd been at it, he'd asked Master Marcus to design some unobtrusive pieces that no one would consider kinky. Now that she was here, David was glad he'd had the foresight to do that. He looked forward to their mutual introduction to Master Marcus' creation.

Earlier in the day, David had moved aside his workout machines and weight bench, leaving the area vacant for their use.

"I don't get it," she said when he came downstairs. "It's a nice space, but…"

"It doesn't look like a dungeon?"

"Not at all."

"Pull that tapestry off the wall."

She did. "Ah. Hmm." She took a step back and studied the pieces of wood attached to the wall. "Interesting." She placed the tapestry on the floor and rolled it up. "Sorry. I still don't get it."

"It serves the same purpose as a St Andrew's cross."

Maggie looked again, closer. "Oh! Clever."

He thought so, too. The structure was about six feet in width and height. Holes were drilled at strategic intervals for placement of hooks, meaning a sub could be attached wherever the Dom desired. Even the individual slats could be removed or not, as David saw fit. Since it didn't have an official name, he called it the Cavendish, in honour of its designer.

"Devious," she added. "No one would ever know it's down here."

He opened the top of a bench — another of Marcus' designs. The furniture had been installed beneath a window. Guests who opened it would find a blanket and a remote control for the television and sound system. The upper tray was removable, and his stash of toys was stored beneath.

"Your personality is like this room, isn't it?" she observed. "You'd never expect what's beneath the exterior."

"I'm the same on the inside and the outside."

"Uh-huh. Sorry, Mr Tomlinson. Not buying it. You are much deeper, more concerned about things and people — me — than you let on."

"You have it wrong, Maggie. I assure you."

"Whatever you say, Sir."

He glanced at her.

"I'm agreeing with you, Mr Tomlinson." She shrugged. "As always."

"You're incorrigible, Maggie."

She flashed him a cheeky grin.

"Would you prefer I flog your back or front?" He nodded, selecting a flogger with broad straps so he could give her a long, sound beating.

Her smile faded, and she took in a sharp breath, not from fear, he sensed, but from unfurling anticipation.

She kept an eye on him as he shook it out. "Whatever Sir prefers," she said.

This time, sincerity was etched in her words.

He laid the implement aside and took out hooks, clamps, ties, restraints, lube and even a medium-sized butt plug.

"I guess you weren't kidding that we wouldn't be watching television," she said.

"Not a chance."

"All that for tonight?"

"Do you have something better to do?"

"Ah. No, Mr Tomlinson."

"Come here, please." He put cuffs on her wrists. They weren't his preferred metal ones, but the fabric ones would work better for his purposes. Not that it really mattered. He just liked having her in them. He knelt to secure a second pair to her ankles. "You'll be helpless in less than five minutes."

"I'm already tied up inside," she said, her voice so soft he hardly heard it.

So was he. He hadn't expected that. He didn't know how to respond. Before he completely lost the ability to think, he picked up four hooks. "Stand with your back against the structure."

In front of him, she looked so small, but he knew how tough she was. She'd taken everything he'd given, and she'd done it with impressive stoicism. "Please raise your arms." He stepped back to look at her relative to the Cavendish then repositioned her. "Now spread your legs. Keep your feet flat on the floor, as I don't want to strain any of your muscles." He repeated the procedure and double-checked each distance before inserting the hooks into pre-drilled holes. "You may step away."

She frowned.

"There are a few things I want to do to you before I start the flogging," he explained. "That was mechanical, and I want you in a different mental state before my leather meets your skin. Let's start with some clamps." He handed her a pair. "Put them on."

"Me? You want me to do it to myself? That seems like you're asking me to tie my own noose."

"You play with this type all the time. Quit stalling."

Without further complaint, she tugged on her left nipple, pinching it, squeezing it.

"I could watch you do that all day."

She continued long after the nipple had hardened.

"You're doing that to aggravate me," he said.

"Not at all. I'm trying to please you, Mr Tomlinson."

"Don't forget who will be holding the flogger."

She looked up at him through her long lashes, but she didn't stop toying with her nipple.

"Put the clamp on it," he snapped, the words almost sounding like a growl.

Rather than being intimidated, she laughed. She squeezed her aureole between her thumb and forefinger of her left hand, making the nipple protrude. He knew she was very much aware of his interest, and she took her sweet time opening the pincer and guiding it towards her nipple.

She placed the clamp and sucked in a shocked breath.

"More than you expected?" he asked.

"Hell and back. Yes, Sir."

"Is it more than you can bear?"

"If it pleases you, Sir, I can take it."

In his pants, his cock felt hot and heavy. Once she stepped away from her inhibitions, her sexual power quadrupled. She could ask for anything and he'd crawl through shards of metal to get it for her.

"Shall I do the other one now, Mr Tomlinson?"

An internal debated raged inside him. Touching her might be lethal. Watching her play with herself would lead him to fuck her before they'd even started. "I'll do it."

The little vixen pouted. Everything she did made his desire rise to flash point.

He followed her lead, plumping her breast, abrading her nipple with his callused fingertip. She moaned and allowed her head to fall backwards. Her hair streamed down her back in waves of untamed abandon.

David pinched her nipple and pulled it away from her body before releasing the clamp to bite it.

She fisted her hands and he saw her fingernails dig into her palms. He considered removing the clovers, but he remained silent and waited for her to use her safe word.

By slow measures, she uncurled her fingers and looked at him. "Thank you, Sir."

This woman was tough, all right. "They won't seem as bad in a while." Until he yanked on them. By then, he hoped she was so far gone in her delirium that she would be able to ignore the pain in favour of its crashing arousal.

With his foot, he slid an exercise mat towards her. "Kneel and present your ass for my plug."

"Of course, Mr Tomlinson," she whispered.

Her movements were beautiful as she stepped onto the mat and knelt. After a glance at him, she lowered herself the rest of the way to the floor, her ass high in the air. He noticed she didn't flatten her breasts. He'd see to that in a minute. "Reach back and spread your ass cheeks for me, Maggie." That forced her to adjust her position a bit, and she yelped.

He kept her waiting while he lubed the piece. He drizzled the excess liquid into the crack between her ass cheeks before teasing her tightest entrance with the blunt end of the plug. "I love doing this to you," he said. "Stretching you. That's it, bear down."

She relaxed her muscles and he inserted the piece a bit more before pulling it out.

"I've never had a glass plug before."

"What do you think?"

"It doesn't give," she said around a grunt as he proceeded to push it back in.

"Not like silicone," he agreed. "Neither does stainless, but this is bigger than the one I used on you at the Den since I intend to fuck you up your ass later."

She shuddered and released her grip on her butt cheeks.

"Compose yourself at once," he snapped.

"*Aww.* God! Sorry, Mr Tomlinson."

"Better," he said when she was back in position. Then showing no mercy, deciding to get it over with, he shoved it the rest of the way in with a gentle but firm glide.

She panted and yelped.

"It's in. Feel free to stop the dramatics." Avoiding her hands, he gave her right buttock a sharp smack to reinforce his words.

He stood and walked around her, admiring the way she looked with her ass in the air, a plug protruding from her anus. Her body was all feminine curves and beauty. "When you're ready, please take your place at the wall."

Her motions were exaggeratedly slow as she stood. The plug and the clamps hampered her movements. That her interest in BDSM matched his was the stuff of fantasies. After Sandy, he'd given up the hope of finding someone who would complement him in bed as well as out of it.

He attached her cuffs to the hooks, spreading her body wide. "Would you like a gag or would you rather scream the house down?"

"Those are big words, Mr Tomlinson."

"I'll back them up." He'd heard the teasing note in her retort. Interesting that he already recognised the difference in her tone when something was bothering her and when she was goading him to give her everything she wanted. "Lower your head and open your mouth."

She drew her eyebrows together but did as she was told. He picked up the chain that dangled between her clamps and placed it between her teeth. "Don't let go."

Her eyes were wide. Every movement would drag on the chain. He hoped it would be an experience she'd never forget. "How are you doing, sub?" he asked, tucking wayward strands of her hair behind her ears.

She murmured something, turning her cheek against his hand for comfort.

He stepped away from her, and she tracked him with her gaze. In that position, she was hobbled and gagged and about to endure something he was willing to bet she'd never dealt with before.

David picked up his flogger and approached her. "Let go of that chain at any time to signal that the scene is too much."

In his cuffs, she formed a circle with her thumb and index finger, indicating everything was okay. "I'll start slow."

With a back-and-forth flicking motion, he flogged her belly and pelvis, shifting his stance so he could catch her already-swollen labia.

She moaned and pulled against the restraints, but she didn't release the chain, and she kept her hand curled in the same position.

He fell into a rhythm as he went up and down her lower torso. She closed her eyes in total surrender. He continued with the same motions, using more or less the same amount of pressure, letting her know what to expect. This was about nothing other than her pleasure.

Then, wanting to strike her breasts with more force and not worry about touching her face, he transferred the multi-strand whip to his left hand. "Let it go," he told her, reaching for the chain.

She did and said, "Thank you."

"Your manners are exquisite." He resumed the beating with more vigour, searing her breasts and jostling the clamps to the point she whimpered from the pain.

Her face flushed and perspiration covered her body.

"You've got some beautiful marks," he said. "You may not see them by Monday, but you'll enjoy them for the rest of the night and, I'm guessing, all of tomorrow." He hadn't paused, and she hadn't asked him to. Rather, she'd allowed her head to rest against the slats behind her.

Was Maggie nearing subspace again, and so fast?

Damn, her ability to shove aside everything else, but the moment astounded him. He understood how this could be cathartic to her, satisfying her in a way that exercise did for him. No wonder she looked forward to her outings at the Den. Subspace wasn't a vague idea to her, it was a destination she headed for.

He kept her there for a while, criss-crossing her body and leaving behind vivid streaks of red. She allowed the restraints to take more of her weight as she leaned into the lashing. He spoke to her non-stop, and two minutes after her last verbal response, he eased off, lengthening the time between blows and softening the impact. "Stay where you are," he told her. "I've got you."

After tossing aside the flogger, he unfastened her ankles, then released her wrists. Her body sagged, and he caught her in his embrace, carrying her up the stairs to the living room. Still holding her, he sat on the couch. He debated what to do about her clamps before deciding to leave them in place. Soon they'd become uncomfortable enough for her to remove them herself.

Smoothing her hair and holding her tight, he matched her breathing. Then, when they were in synch, he led her into a shallower pattern.

She began to stir. He couldn't make out her first words, but it didn't matter. Before long, she reached for the clamps, but she lacked the fine motor skills to release the tips. He brushed aside her hands and removed both at the same time.

"Yowzer," she said, punctuating the word with a short yelp.

"Welcome back."

"You're worse than an alarm clock," she told him. "I'm hitting the snooze button."

He grinned as she settled against him again.

She was quiet for so long, he began to wonder if she was asleep. A few minutes later she said, "That was spectacular."

"I'm glad you enjoyed it. So did I. No real lingering pain from the beating?"

"Not at all. My body feels like it's glowing," she said. "This might sound odd, but I'm relaxed, and I'm invigorated at the same time."

"Go on."

"I don't go there all the time, but I like to. You're particularly skilled at what you do." She looked at him. "I think I had my eyes closed during the flogging."

"You did."

"It's strange."

She stopped and started, explaining things in fragments, and he allowed her to talk at her own pace without interruption.

"Once I stop fighting, let my body accept it, everything seemed brighter. Not just light, but a blinding white. Sounds... They seem to be a million miles away. I hear you when you say my name. But otherwise... The real world has no distinction. I guess it's like being in a swimming pool." She was silent before adding. "Thank you for the experience."

"Pleasing you matters to me, Maggie mine."

She was quiet again for a long time, and he skimmed a thin red stripe that marred her shoulder.

"I think I should buy stock in a company that manufactures arnica."

"I don't mind skipping it."

"Sorry. That's not an option."

"I want to keep a couple of marks so I can remember the experience."

And get her through the time to the next scene? "We can talk about that. But I won't have you walking around with painful bruises."

"Spoilsport, Mr Tomlinson."

"A Dom, Ms Carpenter. Your Dom."

She exhaled a long-suffering sigh and protested, "Just because you have me in a collar —"

"And cuffs."

"And cuffs," she repeated.

"And in my house."

"Are you done yet?" She pursed her lips. "None of that means you get to boss me around."

"Yes. I'm afraid it does."

She looked up and dug her hand into his hair. It was her first real, intimate gesture, and it meant something powerful to him. She trailed her fingers down his cheekbone and settled on his chin. "You're insufferable, Sir."

Insufferable enough, evidently, for her to move her hand lower to stroke his biceps.

"I'm glad," she admitted.

He raised his eyebrows.

"There's a certain comfort in that," she said. "Which I wouldn't admit if I hadn't had that wonderful experience. If you bring it up again, I'll deny I said it."

"I wouldn't expect anything else from you."

"Keep that arm in flogging order for me, will you?"

"Your wish is my command, princess."

"Do you need arnica for your wrist?"

"After your next spanking, I might." He upended her, tossing her over his lap.

"You wouldn't!" She brought her hands back to protect her butt.

He swatted them aside, and before she could protest, he plucked the plug from her anus.

"That was diabolical."

"That averted a pointless debate," he countered. He eased her from his lap and went into the powder room. He brought back a washcloth and cleansed her before returning to the bathroom.

"I'm not sure I'll ever get over you doing that for me," she confessed as he sat next to her and held her close again, mindful that she didn't catch a chill now that her body was cooling.

"You said that as if you think you have any say in the matter."

"Mr Tomlinson—"

"Master," he corrected. "Master David." In his arms, she froze. Time seemed to teeter on a precipice of disaster.

"I... Ah..."

He breathed out and the moment lurched forwards.

"You have no issue with using the title when you address Master Damien, or other Doms for that matter. I won't demand it of you, but when you're ready to show the courtesy, it will be well-received."

"I'm not sure what to say. I mean no disrespect, but Mr Tomlinson seems unique and fitting." She raised her palms as if beseeching him to understand. "It's what I call you. To me, it is a term of respect. At the beginning..." She looked away. "Damn, I feel bad saying this... In the beginning, maybe it wasn't. But it is now. When we're alone, it's..." She seemed to stumble for the word. "Different. I'm not making myself understood, but the distinction is clear in my mind."

"I concede your point."

"But it still matters to you?"

"I'll give it some consideration."

She scooted onto her knees and kissed him. Who knew this side of Maggie even existed? "I'm curious, with the way you want to be dominated, why aren't you in a permanent BDSM relationship?"

"It's complicated. All relationships are, right? I love my work, and since I joined the firm, a lot of my time has been taken up with that. Most men in my social circle are scandalised by any suggestion that I want to be hurt in any way. Doms... You can be a demanding bunch. I'm not sure I'm up for the constant battle. I want my kink in the bedroom, so I participate in a series of scenes that I keep confined to weekends. That works best for me."

"The event I'd been watching you mark off on your desk calendar. That was the night at the Den?"

"I had today circled, too," she said.

That pumped up his ego. A nice change from the way she usually deflated it. He thought about that calendar, with every detail of her life jotted in blue ink. "Is there a date circled for your next outing?"

"I put the ladies' nights on there as soon as Gregorio sends the announcements," she said. "Vanessa and I almost always go."

The sensation of being knocked back a step was as unexpected as it was unwelcome. Did she have no regard for the fact he was human? "You won't be attending."

"Excuse me? That's not part of our arrangement."

"It is now."

"Did your report cards in school have notes that you don't play well with others?"

"Don't tempt fate, Maggie," he warned. No way was he turning her delectable ass over to another Dom for a beating. David wasn't a possessive man, but from the moment he'd seen her as a submissive, he'd wanted her in his cuffs. "If I'm the one you're turning to, I'll make sure you want for nothing. Go out with your friends somewhere else."

"I'm just looking for someone to spank me."

"And you walked into my office and offered me the position." He held her tighter. "Yield to me, Maggie mine." For long moments, she kept herself stiff. "You don't have to fight me on every issue."

"I don't want us to move too fast."

"We're not. We're simply outlining where the boundaries are."

Maggie remained where she was without pulling away, and that spoke volumes to him. That she continued to stay instead of choosing to go home when he suggested they light a fire in the outdoor pit as the sun set, spoke even louder.

"Sounds nice," she said.

"I'll get you one of my flannel shirts. And a refill on the wine?" He didn't let his subs drink much, but over the course of the day, she'd hadn't even consumed a full glass.

"No, thanks."

He got her the shirt, and she rolled up the sleeves to her elbows. She only fastened the top button. Somehow, in his clothing, she looked smaller and more vulnerable. Something about Maggie made him want to wrap her up and protect her, fight her battles, see to her safety.

They went outside and she sat on a bench, knees pulled to her chest as she watched him place the wood and ignite it.

She scooted over and he sat next to her as the fire settled in.

"What about you?" she asked. "Why are you single?"

"I was married once. I accept the responsibility for the failure. I didn't give her the time she needed or deserved." He looked at Maggie intently. "I've learnt from my mistakes. Anything worth having is worth investing in. It doesn't mean it's easy, and it doesn't mean it won't take work."

She didn't respond, and neither of them seemed to have a need to break the silence. He enjoyed her companionship. For a long time after his divorce, he'd enjoyed his solitude. Now that Maggie was with him, he didn't want to let her go.

"We didn't have sex earlier," she said much later, turning to face him.

The dim light made it difficult to read her expression, but her unspoken meaning was clear.

"I mean, after we left your basement."

"I've been acting like a gentleman and giving you time to recover."

"Would you quit that?" she asked.

"You'd rather I act like a Neanderthal?"

"Yes, please." She grinned.

"A woman after my heart." He stood and offered his hand, accepting her unspoken invitation. "I've wanted to fuck you up the ass all day."

Chapter Eight

No matter what Maggie was expecting David to say, he almost always shocked her. She didn't have a lot of experience with anal sex. Plugs, yes. But an actual dick—an enormous one at that—not so much. The realisation he intended to pound her made her feel submissive and feminine.

She slid her hand against his and revelled in his raw, masculine strength as he pulled her to her feet. It was a wonder, really, that he possessed all that power, but used the perfect amount to arouse her without crossing the line.

Maggie had no idea how long he'd flogged her earlier. Once the first blow had landed on her body, she'd surrendered to him. No. That wasn't the truth. From the moment she'd arrived, she'd given him all her trust.

He'd taken exquisite care of her, giving her what she'd wanted and bringing her back when she was so lost that pain and pleasure merged into indistinguishable bliss.

She wondered what would happen if she extended that trust to other areas of their relationship as he seemed to want, both at work and in private. Doing so would mean she'd be more exposed emotionally, open to being hurt.

Since her father had died when she was so young and her mother had her own issues to deal with, Maggie had learnt to rely on herself. Her other relationships had offered her little incentive to modify that behaviour. She was so set in her ways that she wasn't sure it was possible to change. It surprised her that she was even considering it.

He held her hand as they walked inside, and he shut the door behind them before releasing her. She looked up at him as he unfastened her button then shucked the shirt from her shoulders. "Back to being naked, Sir?"

"Sorry, Maggie. It's been at least a week since I've seen your breasts."

"You mean an hour or two, Mr Tomlinson."

"Seems like a week."

The material slipped to the floor. She pulled back her shoulders and arched her back. He rolled each nipple between his thumb and forefinger. Now she had no idea why she'd protested when he insisted she stay naked. Each time he touched her, an illicit thrill shot through her. That she'd been clamped with such vicious pincers earlier only magnified his effect.

Under his careful, firm touch, her pussy started to moisten. It was frightening how masterfully he aroused her.

"The bedroom, now," he urged, "before I bugger you here."

"I..." She couldn't believe the thought that went through her mind. When he looked at her with his eyebrows drawn together, she hurried through her suggestion. "The stairs might be interesting."

"Good God."

"I mean, we don't have to. Never mind. That was a strange idea."

"I should have thought of it myself," he disagreed. "I'll be back with the lube."

Maggie wondered if she'd lost her mind. A bed made much more sense. But damn, the first time she'd looked at those polished wooden steps, she'd thought of wild monkey sex on them. Since the staircase was crafted from individual boards, it would be easy for her to hold on. The potential positions he could put her in were endless.

In addition to the bottle of lube, he returned with a damp washcloth and a dry hand towel as well as a condom. Always prepared. She desired him, his domination and possession. He wasn't gentle, giving her the exact right amount of roughness. "I want your dick in my mouth first. If I may, Sir."

Beneath his casual black pants, she saw his cock was already thick. Though she'd sucked cock before, she had almost always considered it something she was required to do. But she'd had him in her mouth that first night at the Den, and she had a real desire to taste him again.

Without waiting for his approval, she knelt while he toed off his sandals. She drew his pants down and he kicked them away.

She inhaled the scent of him before leaning in to lick his sac then suck each ball, one at a time, into her mouth. He groaned and reached for her, digging his hands into her hair. The slight tug let her know how much he appreciated her efforts.

Emboldened, she reached for his cock and licked her way up the shaft. She closed her mouth around the head and pressed her tongue against the underneath, seeing the way he jerked his hips in response. She loved pleasing him. Moving her hand as well as her mouth, she worked him, making him moan. Her pussy flooded with moisture, and it surprised her that she could become so turned on just from tasting him.

David imprisoned her head and held her so that he was able to control how deep she took him. That alone showed her his natural dominance. He would never cede control to her, not that she wanted him to.

That realisation made her pause for a second. She'd said as much to him earlier, when she'd confessed she didn't always mind him being in charge. But more and more, she was not only admitting it, she was accepting it.

Feeling his hand press on the back of her head, she resumed the blow job, shoving aside her thoughts and concentrating on him.

"Nice," he approved.

She continued trying to take him all the way to his root. She choked a little, and he pulled back while releasing his grip on her hair.

"We can try that again another time," he said as her eyes watered.

"That wasn't what I meant to have happen," she said, wiping her face with the back of her hand.

"I appreciate your trying," he assured her. "As for now, let's get you ready. Show me your ass."

Since she was already kneeling, it didn't take much to get on all fours and raise her rear end as high as she could. Without being instructed, she knew to reach back and part her buttocks.

"That is a nice view, Maggie."

She felt a slight pressure against her ass hole. She was tender from the glass plug he'd used earlier, but as he fingered her hole, he used plenty of lubricant and she began to relax, giving him access.

"What a good princess."

As a result of their previous play, she wasn't as tight as normal. He went deeper, stretching her as he did. When he slid in a second digit, she grunted, a very unladylike sound that made him laugh.

"Now a third," he said.

Without his coaching, she swayed backwards, easing his way.

"That should about do it," he said.

He wiped his hands before he said, "Crawl over to the staircase."

The longer she was with him, the less self-conscious she felt. Her long-term exposure to the BDSM lifestyle had left her without many body-image issues. If she wanted her ample bottom to get spanked, there wasn't much point in hiding it. But under his constant attention mixed with approval, her confidence blossomed. She knew he found her sexy and she got a thrill from the knowledge she possessed the ability to arouse him by how she moved her body.

With an exaggerated sway of her hips, she sashayed across the hardwood floors. She started up the stairs and stopped when he told her to.

She looked back at him. At some point he'd discarded his shirt. He was glorious in his nakedness. It was a good thing he kept his clothes on for the most part. Seeing him with an insistent erection scrambled her brains. Knowing it would soon be inside her stole her breath.

Her mouth dried as he rolled the condom down his length then covered it in plenty of lube.

He didn't walk towards her, he stalked her as if she were prey. His jaw was set, and his deep blue eyes pulsed with electric energy.

Maggie took a couple of deep, steadying breaths. She expected him to force his cockhead against her, but he didn't. Instead, he went behind her and slid his hands between her legs. He teased her pussy, finger-fucking her while pressing against her clitoris.

He tantalised and thrilled until she cried out for more. "In me," she said between pants. "I want you in me."

Only then did he press himself against her whorl.

"Hold on," he warned her. "If at any time the angle is too much, say so. The stairs could make this tricky."

"I love it." And she did. This gave him a different position, and she held onto two separate stairs for greater stability which allowed her to thrust her hips backwards.

He entered her in a series of ever-deepening thrusts, giving her an opportunity to adjust. Still, the anal penetration hurt a bit. She preferred the feel of his masculine flesh to that of the impermeable glass, but he was still bigger in circumference than the plug had been.

"So fucking tight."

She hadn't heard that tone from him before, rough and edgy. And it emboldened her. She exhaled and pushed back when he surged forwards. "Do it," she said. "Fuck me, Mr Tomlinson."

He grasped her hips, pulling her against his pelvis as he forced his dick the remainder of the way in.

She cried out.

"Damn," he said. He moved a hand to rub one of her shoulders. "Are you okay?"

"It's… Full. Overwhelming."

"Is that good or bad?"

"Good." Now that she'd adjusted, she liked it.

"Thank God," he said. "I'd stop, but hell if I want to."

He pulled out to his cockhead before he eased back in.

After several dozen sensuous strokes, each more overwhelming than the last, he spoke. "I want to try something different. I'm going to help you to stand. Are you willing to try?"

She doubted the possibility that they'd be able to pull it off, but she didn't tell him that. He reached an arm around her and braced her chest.

"Lean back."

The added danger made her pulse race. "Slipping would suck, Sir."

"I've got you, Maggie."

She reached behind her and wrapped an arm around his neck, feeling more secure. "Christ," she said as the angle changed and he went even deeper.

Behind her, he bent his knees, using her body to jerk himself off. Over and over, she cried out. The pleasure was unimaginable, but it came from the sensation of being torn apart for her lover.

"I'm going to come," he said viciously against her ear.

She wasn't sure how long she could stay in position with her back bent at that angle and her ass stuffed full of cock.

He thrust harder, shattering her, making her orgasm—something she hadn't known was possible from anal sex.

With a masculine, guttural groan, he yanked her back a final time, imprisoning her upper body as he surged forwards and pulsed out his ejaculation.

He kept hold of her for several seconds before slowly releasing her. She lowered her arm then, having no support, she went limp. More mindful than she was, he lowered her to the stairs where she placed her hands.

"Damn," he said, withdrawing his spent penis from her. "Better than I would have imagined." He brushed her hair aside. "I was rougher with you than I'd planned."

"Lucky for us both, I'm not delicate," she replied, though it took several breaths before her head stopped spinning.

He patted her with the damp washcloth. "Can you make it up the stairs or should I carry you?"

"I can walk. Or crawl." She thought about it then added, "At least I think I can."

Somehow she made it upstairs and into the shower with him.

Afterwards, he dried her off, and she stood still, her lips pressed together while he dabbed the white cream on her skin. He'd threatened to withhold all beatings until she was healed if she uttered one word of protest. His tone had been fierce, so she was sure he meant what he said.

When he pulled her against him in the bed, she didn't fight. He kissed the top of her head once again and she fell asleep, only to wake the next morning to the realisation he'd kept her bad dreams at bay.

He climbed from the bed and pulled on a fresh pair of lightweight pants, this time in grey. The fabric allowed her to see that he was already semi-interested. She couldn't wait for him to take her again. Her pussy and ass throbbed from his use, but that only made her want more. "Is there coffee in my future?" she asked.

"Even a latte if you want it."

"Wait. Did I die and go to heaven?"

"I'll hope you think so. You're having it in the hot tub. Your muscles will appreciate it after yesterday's acrobatics."

"Limbering me up for today's shenanigans?"

"Ah." He pantomimed twirling a moustache. "You're onto my nefarious plot."

Laughing at him, she pulled a pillow against her chest. It had been a long time since she'd enjoyed waking up with a man this much.

"You're welcome to stay in bed while I make your drink."

"I'll freshen up then be down."

He nodded. "I don't need to remind you I expect you to be naked, do I?"

"No, Sir." At every juncture, he reinforced their roles. The surprise was, it didn't chafe.

With a quick nod, he left the room.

By the time she entered the kitchen, her latte was in an unbreakable mug on the counter. He was outside, in the tub. Jets made the water turbulent, and she accepted his hand as she balanced the cup while descending the stairs. "This is quite the way to wake up," she said, looking at the Rockies in the distance.

"It's better when there's someone to share it."

"I would have thought you'd prefer peace and quiet."

"Certain sounds beat the hell out of silence. Your whimpers for one. Your screams for another. And yes, you do scream so don't bother denying it."

"Well then." She sat back and took a sip of her latte. "Damn. You could bring one to the office for me every day."

"You have to come and get them," he said.

"You're a tempting man, Mr Tomlinson." She took a second drink before sliding the cup onto the deck behind her.

"Anytime, Maggie."

He sounded as if he meant it.

"How does your body feel?"

"Horny." She grinned.

"In that case, after breakfast, I'll cuff you to the Cavendish."

"Cavendish? Is that what you're calling your kinky apparatus?"

"It is."

Less than an hour later, he had her spread wide, arms above her head, cuffed to the Cavendish, facing away from him. He'd stripped off his clothes and put on a condom. The scent of her heat already hung on the air. He could turn her on without touching her.

She craned her head to see what he was selecting from the toy box. She winced, wishing she hadn't seen anything when her gaze fixed on a single tail. With that thing, there would be no subspace for her, she knew. But it might leave a mark.

She closed her eyes as she heard him test snap the leather.

Her mouth dried, and for the first time, she considered using her slow word. This was going to hurt.

"You'll manage," he said.

At least that's what she thought he said. Over the sound of the blood rushing in her ears, she could hear little else.

The lash caught her thighs and wrapped around to sear again. *Fuck.* She yanked at her restraints, fighting the agony.

He waited for what seemed a long time while she fought for breath.

Before she was ready, he landed another.

She bounced her heels off the ground, trying to help dissipate the sensation, but it didn't help. This wasn't a spanking, nothing close to it.

He struck her several more times in quick succession, and she did scream. No matter how she tugged and struggled to get away, she was helpless in his cuffs.

"So beautiful."

She hadn't been aware of it, but the whipping had ended. He pressed his cool body against her heated one, forcing her into the structure. He entered her pussy in one powerful thrust.

"You were made for this, sub," he said against her ear as he bent his knees to gain leverage to surge up into her.

Maggie cried out again and again as he rammed her, impaling her against the wall.

"Do you want to come, Maggie?"

"Yes, yes, yes. Please, please, please. *Sir.*" Every part of her vibrated with the need for him to possess her. Her legs and buttocks burnt as if he'd branded her. But damn, the intensity made an orgasm claw at her. "Fuck me. Let me come."

He wrapped his arms around her waist and pounded her. Nothing soft or gentle. Just a raw and primal pulse.

She babbled incoherently, shamelessly moving her body to take him deeper.

"Tight, hot cunt," he said.

"Yours," she said with a gasp.

"Come for me."

She lifted onto her toes and he surged into her again. She felt shredded as she bucked, her pussy convulsing with her orgasm.

She whimpered as he ejaculated.

He dropped his head onto her arm, a revealingly intimate gesture. Part of her wanted the moment to last forever. All too soon, he pulled away, and she felt the physical distance between them. The interlude would end and they'd both return to work tomorrow — she had no idea what that meant for them. Last night he'd been clear that he wanted a personal relationship with her. She'd been trying to convince herself that she could compartmentalise her life. Maggie was no longer as certain.

David unfastened her from the structure then removed the cuffs and collar. She thought it was in some way symbolic, but suspected he wouldn't agree.

"You'll have at least two marks from that," he told her. "No matter how much cream I put on them."

After they'd had lunch on the deck, she put her clothes back on. He walked her to her car and lifted her skirt to swat her butt, reigniting the pain before she got into the car.

Feeling awkward, she drove away without saying goodbye. On the way home, she kept her phone close in case he called or sent a message. He didn't.

* * * *

That night, the bad dreams found her. When she summoned up her inner warrior and turned towards the blue-eyed monster, he vanished, leaving her alone. That chilled her, and she sat up with a start.

Unable to shake the vestiges, she got up earlier than normal and took her coffee onto her small patio to watch the sunrise.

She shifted in her chair, uncomfortable from one of his stripes. Mr Tomlinson's. Master David.

In such a short amount of time, he'd demolished the blocks she had in place to keep him at bay. Sceneing with him had been disastrous to her equilibrium. She'd avoided BDSM relationships because she wanted to be a bedroom slut, not adopt the lifestyle. But he'd made his position clear when he'd stripped her of her clothing, told her she could not attend the ladies' night functions at the Den then asked her to call him Master.

She put down the cup before she sloshed her coffee over the rim. Her worst fear was realised. The more she got, the more she wanted.

By the time she entered the office, she was no closer to figuring out how she'd behave when she saw him at work today.

"Did you have a good weekend, Mags?" Barb asked.

"It was uneventful," she lied. "How was yours?"

"Saw a play for my mom's birthday. Strolled the Sixteenth Street Mall and had too many drinks at a rooftop bar in LoDo."

"With your mother?"

"Woman can put away the vodka."

"You should introduce her to Gloria."

Who, evidently having heard voices, breezed out of her office. Today she had on a turquoise pantsuit with a multi-coloured blouse topped with a contrasting scarf that should have clashed but didn't. The drink in her cup was a shade of purple not found in nature.

"You're here early, Mother."

"We're meeting with the Arctic Fox people today. Did you forget?"

The company designed cold-weather gear for the least habitable places on earth and they were planning to open their first US store in the trendy Larimer Square area. World Wide Now was competing with several other companies to land the opening. They were having an informal sit-down with some of the higher-ups to get a better feel for their ideas. "Anything I can do to help?"

"Make sure the tyrant shows up. They want to meet him."

"I'm putting my foot down. Unless David is out of line, no more calling him names behind his back. He heard us the other day, and it's unfair. Agreed?"

It appeared Gloria tried to frown, but apart from the pursed lips, it was hard to tell. "You got more injections in your face," Maggie said.

"You should both go with me. Dr Smythe knows all the tricks to keeping us looking young. Maybe we could get a group discount."

Barb choked on her coffee. "Not for me, thanks."

"Let's get back to my point," Maggie said. "I'm serious. There will be no more bad-mouthing the boss. We have to set the example around here."

"I think you need a cup of coffee, dear. See if Barb will let you use some of her nice creamer," Gloria said as she grabbed her drink and walked off, jewellery jangling.

Maggie sighed. "It's going to be a long day."

"Sorry about calling David names. Embarrassing that he overheard."

"You know, he might not be as bad as I thought."

"Skip the coffee," Barb said. "I'll call an ambulance. Obviously you're not feeling well."

Shaking her head, Maggie went to her office to finalise details for Friday afternoon's open house and to send David a reminder about their upcoming visitors. She could have asked Barb to touch base with him, but Maggie wanted to handle it herself.

David showed up for the Arctic Fox meet and greet and impressed the VP of Marketing. After the meeting, the two of them moved to the far end of the conference room while Maggie and her mother chatted with two members of the creative team.

A few minutes later, David and the female VP excused themselves, saying they were going out to lunch. She frowned, and David inclined his head, letting her know he'd noticed her displeasure. What the hell was wrong with her? He could eat meals with whomever he wanted.

She didn't see him the rest of the day, and that evening she traced the single welt his whip had left behind. A thousand emotions splintered inside her. She masturbated in the shower, resting her forehead on the tiles as she thought of him.

Since he hadn't contacted her today, she knew it was up to her to approach him again.

* * * *

Maggie had another fitful night and got to the office late.

Her mother was wringing her hands near the reception desk, and Barb had a hand on Gloria's shoulder. "What's going on?"

"I screwed up," Gloria said. Her shoulders started to shake.

"Whatever it is, we can fix it. We always have," Maggie said, trying to keep calm and not disturb the rest of the staff.

"That's what I've been telling her," Barb added.

"Let's go in my office." Where they could close the door. "Is David in yet?" she asked Barb.

"He's at an offsite meeting. I think he'll be in around eleven."

"Thanks." He didn't need to see this side of her mother, either. After nodding her thanks to Barb, Maggie drew Gloria down the hall. "Have a seat," she said when they were in the office. Maggie sat on the edge of her desk.

Gloria sat and dropped her head into her hands.

Maggie waited for minute before gently saying, "I can only help if I know what's wrong."

"I got so caught up with Arctic Fox that I forgot to send the paperwork through on the Hoskins Group deal."

Maggie froze.

When her mother looked up, Maggie blinked, trying not to betray her raw panic. Cindy Hoskins owned six different businesses, and World Wide Now handled four of the accounts. For years, they'd been trying to land all six, offering screaming discounts for the additional business. Cindy Hoskins was a pragmatist who didn't believe in a single vendor approach. But losing the four accounts existing would be costly.

Maggie forced herself to breathe. "Surely it's not that bad. When was it due?"

"Last Thursday."

"Why wasn't it on the board?"

Her mother dropped her head again.

"Okay, never mind that. We'll remedy it in future."

"I took them the preliminary bid two weeks ago and..."

Didn't follow up. "Let me see what I can do." She picked up the phone and dialled Cindy's office direct, throwing herself on the other woman's mercy. Cindy agreed to reconsider, as long as she had the signed deal in hand before noon.

Maggie summoned Barb to print off a final copy of the contract from the server. The three of them went over it. There weren't many changes from the previous year, but there wasn't time to figure in an annual increase.

David would be livid that his procedures hadn't been followed.

Reluctant to bring him into the conversation, she called his cellular, but it went straight to voicemail. "Crap, crap, crap."

"Think, think, think," urged Barb.

Having no other choice, she signed two copies of the contract and put them in an envelope before heading out of the door.

She walked the six blocks to the bank building where the Hoskins Group was headquartered and, with a sigh and a smile, handed the envelope to the receptionist.

When she got back to the office she found frozen drinks waiting for everyone, courtesy of Gloria. When she created buckets of drama, she liked to treat the survivors.

Maggie didn't see David until the next day. She considered mentioning the Hoskins Group fiasco, but didn't. She and the team had sat down to discuss ways to ensure something like that never happened again. David was a big believer in systems, and they'd refined theirs as a result. Barb went through all the client files and entered all contract renewal dates in the computer and set several reminders beginning a month in advance.

"Go home with me Friday night after the open house," he said.

Startled, she looked up from her keyboard. "David."

He lazed against the doorjamb as if he owned the place. Which, really, he did.

"Don't tell me you don't need a beating."

"Yeah." She dropped her hands to her lap. "I do."

"You'll be ready for the hot tub and a good night's sleep."

"That obvious, huh?"

"Only to someone who's looking. You're a beautiful woman, Maggie. Wear something short to the open house." Without another word, he pushed away from the wooden frame and continued down the hall.

She could have sworn she heard him whistle.

Maggie collapsed against her chair back. He'd undone all her resolve in less than a minute. Now she was thinking about him and Friday night instead of work.

* * * *

At home, she masturbated again, this time driven by fantasies of what might happen over the weekend.

Thursday, she worked late, double-checking RSVPs and responding to a few last-minute stragglers. One person asked for directions, even though she'd given them twice. She sent an updated head count to the caterer and glanced at her handwritten to-do list. Everyone else used a computer programme, but there was nothing she liked better than the tactile sensation of marking through a task she'd completed. It was much the same high that she got when she crossed through dates on a calendar, like when she was going to the Den.

The phone rang, and since Barb had already left, she went to answer it. She frowned when she saw David's line light up. It wasn't unusual for him to take a call, she just hadn't realised he was still in the office.

She was cleaning off her desk when he entered her office. She felt his overwhelming presence even before he spoke. He commanded the space and her attention. "David." Instead of a smile, a storm was gathered in his blue eyes, darkening them by several shades.

"That was Cindy Hoskins RSVP'ing for our open house."

Her heart stuttered.

"Something you'd like to tell me about?"

She wondered how much he knew. Then she sighed, realising it didn't matter. He could never trust a woman who hid anything, and she'd already committed a huge gaffe. "We had an issue with a contract not being delivered on time. I chatted with Cindy, asked for an extension, and we offered them the same terms as last year. I got the contract over to her, and the copy with her original signature arrived today." She picked up a pen and toyed with it. The same pen she'd used to sign the document in his stead.

"At what point were you going to tell me?"

She met his gaze. "I wasn't."

"Thank you for your honesty." Without another word, he left. He didn't ask for explanations or lose his temper. In fact, his control gave her goosebumps.

Just then, she acknowledged how badly she'd screwed up. She had tried to reach him by phone, but the missed connection was no reason to have kept quiet. To him, siding with her mother and covering the situation up must feel like a betrayal.

She dropped the pen.

At first, she cloaked herself in righteous indignation. He was overreacting. This was why they shouldn't have got involved. Her business decision should feel like that, nothing more serious. In fact, she had told him she didn't want a BDSM relationship, just to play in the bedroom.

Then she admitted the truth, in agreeing to go home with him tomorrow night, they were in a relationship. She thought of him, remembered him, fantasised about him.

He'd placed her in a position of trust in his organisation when he could have brought in his own people. He'd kept on her mother and had done his best to help her flourish, and now he was brokering a deal with another company so her mom's dream could become an even bigger reality.

She'd thought she was brave by putting a stop to the name-calling. In actuality, she should have done that months before.

He wasn't the one who had ever mixed things up. She was.

Could it be any worse? She took a drink of water for courage before walking to his office. His door was closed, so she knocked. She turned the knob and peeked in when he didn't answer. He was sitting with his back to the door, staring out of the window. "Can I come in?" she asked.

"No, Maggie. I'd prefer you didn't."

"I'd like to talk."

"I wouldn't."

She trembled as she pulled the door closed. In her office, she stalled, hoping he'd relent and come after her, but he didn't.

All night, she kept her phone next to her, waking up every hour to check the screen.

There was no contact, and, as she got ready the following day, she had no idea how to dress. David had told her to wear a short skirt. He'd also invited her to spend the night. She was sure that wasn't happening, since he hadn't said a word to her after he'd refused to invite her into his office.

She opted for her usual wear, pretending her soul didn't feel fractured.

Pain split her head, made worse by the several blocks' walk from her car. When she entered the front door, she headed straight for the medicine cabinet in the break room. She downed two aspirin with the black coffee Barb poured.

"Too much fun last night?"

Maggie shook her head, and even that hurt. "Not enough sleep."

The morning passed in a blur of activity as the caterers arrived and centrepieces and new marketing pieces were delivered. She instructed an intern on how to set up the booth they used for trade shows, and the IT techs tested their projectors.

A copywriter entered her office and handed her the final script they'd be using during the announcements to ensure they thanked everyone who was there. He also handed her David's bio to use when she introduced him as the new owner.

Gloria swooped in wearing a red maxi dress with at least three metal belts wrapped around her waist. "Things are looking good. You've done a great job on the organisation, and I understand all of our biggest clients will be here. I just hope the tyrant can be bothered to show up during his part."

"Out." Maggie pointed at the door.

"What do you mean?"

"I warned you that I won't listen to that. Go find someone else who will. And if they do, I'll fire them. It's insidious and it stops now. Here."

"I never," Gloria protested.

"Yeah, you did. Never gave him a chance, and neither did I. You've got a fat pay cheque coming that you wouldn't have had otherwise." And still might not if he chose to fire her for insubordination. She wouldn't blame him if he did. "You might try a little cooperation when all else fails." She knew that, to others, he might not look engaged because he spent so much time working offsite on the other deal. But speculation about his work hours had to end too, particularly when almost everyone at World Wide Now set their own schedules.

One of the catering assistants popped her head in the door. "I don't know where you'd like the cake?"

Maggie wondered if it would be rude to cut a piece and eat it now. She could use the sugar boost. "Mother, can you help her?"

"This way," Gloria said to the young lady, once again distracted. "The frosting doesn't have dairy, does it?"

David showed up, dapper in grey with a blue tie. Wildly she wondered if that was the one he'd shoved in her mouth the first night at her condo.

"You've done a nice job on the event," he told her. "I understand you got my bio?"

"Gloria will be reading it, if that's all right?"

He nodded.

"You can do the acknowledgements. I thought I'd handle the welcome and the staff introductions. You up for a rehearsal?"

He nodded again.

They had a large presentation room and, except for a couple of bar-height tables, it had been cleared.

Their sound person joined them, showed them how the lapel microphones worked, ran through a check then stepped back while Maggie, Gloria and David read through their lines.

"We make a good team," Gloria said.

By the time David's introduction had been made to the crowd, Maggie agreed. When they worked together, things ran seamlessly. David even displayed some unexpected humour that caught some laughter and a smattering of applause.

She stayed through the end. And went home alone.

He hadn't even stuck around to say goodnight.

What had she expected? She swallowed the lump in her throat. How could she have been so shallow? David had been open, if unyielding, about his expectations of her. There weren't many. He even cooked and made Sunday-morning lattes.

She'd been so caught up in looking at the situation through fearful eyes that she'd blown her chance to be with the one man who satisfied her more than anyone ever had. He would have continually pushed her, but the rewards she'd already experienced were more than she could have imagined.

Feeling miserable, she picked up the phone and asked Vanessa to join her for a drink. Vanessa said she had only a little time before her two men were coming over. "I'll share," Vanessa added.

"I'll pass. Thanks."

"Come on over, I'll make you a margarita. You don't have to stay."

She swung by Vanessa's but just felt more miserable when the first taste of salt hit her tongue. She wasn't in the mood to be cheered up. What should had been a celebratory evening following the mad success of the open house had ended up echoing with loneliness, amplified by Vanessa's uncontained enthusiasm for her night ahead.

When the hunks in leather pants and no shirts arrived, Maggie excused herself.

"Not tempted?" Vanessa asked.

"Not even a little bit."

"You've got it bad," Vanessa said. "We'll go shopping tomorrow."

One of the guys grabbed Vanessa's hair and pulled back her head.

"If you survive," Maggie said with a grin. She let herself out and went home alone.

Chapter Nine

"Has anyone seen my sanity?" Maggie asked the next Friday morning as she accepted one of the frozen drinks Barb had brought in. "I lost it somewhere." She stabbed a straw through the lid and took a grateful sip. Cold caffeine laced with chocolate hit her system, providing a much needed jolt. Not sleeping well for almost two weeks had caught up with her, leaving her mentally and emotionally weak. She'd worked dozens of extra hours, trying to stay busy and hoping David would finally speak to her.

"Did you look in the break room?" Barb asked. "Maybe it's in that box of pastries. That's where I found mine."

"Pastries?" Gloria asked. She'd refused one of the milk-based drinks, but her tone went up an octave at the mention of sweets. "Any maple doughnuts?"

"I don't know. I saw something with sprinkles, though."

Gloria walked away.

"Will you bring me a petit four?" Barb called. "It will be my second," she admitted to Maggie. "They're so small, I figure I can eat about eight and only equal one piece of cake. Right?"

"I don't judge."

The front door opened and David walked in.

Breath vaporised in Maggie's lungs. How was it possible for him to devastate her more every day?

His tailored navy blue suit emphasised the breadth of his shoulders and the colour of his eyes. His hair was getting longer, more rakish. He smelt shower-fresh, with a layer of masculine prowess.

"Morning, ladies."

"I've got an extra chocolate caramel upside down latte, if you want it," Barb said.

"I'll just stick with coffee. Thanks," he said.

Was Maggie the only one who felt the sizzling charge in the atmosphere?

He nodded and moved past her. She caught a glimpse of his supple leather belt and an erotic chill danced down her spine.

"Does he seem different to you?" Barb asked.

"In what way?"

"I don't know, more distant." Barb accepted the tiny pastry Gloria carried in. "I was just asking Mags if she thinks David seems different," she said, including Gloria in the conversation.

"He's always polite," Gloria said. "In a frosty kind of way. He's never given me the time of day. But I get what you mean. He spends more time in his office with the door closed than he ever has."

At least Gloria was no longer making snide comments about his work habits. It would take a while for her to come around, but it was a start.

"See what I mean?" Barb asked.

Gloria sank her teeth into an éclair. "Damn, this is good."

"I'm sure he's fine," Maggie said.

"We're all being nicer and more respectful, like you told us to, but he seems to have become more remote. Maybe you could ask him if there's something wrong," Barb suggested.

"Me?" Maggie asked, horrified.

"He talks to you more than the rest of us."

"Not true." *Not anymore.*

"It's true," Gloria disagreed. "You work more closely with him than anyone does."

"Find out, Mags."

She nodded since she couldn't out-and-out lie.

"I need to check my email," Gloria said as she licked cream from her finger and headed for her office.

"You didn't tell her the filling is dairy," Barb said.

"You tell her," Maggie replied. "If you want me to talk to David, you have to deal with her. Only fair."

"I guess both of us are keeping our mouths shut then?" Barb said with a grin, reaching for her treat.

She had a meeting with David to show him revisions to the new company's logo. Even though he'd approved the eagle previously, she'd had one of the lines removed so that the talons appeared fiercer. It complemented the more streamlined lettering of the company name.

"I like it." He signed his initials to the bottom of the page. "We're still keeping it under wraps?"

"Of course." It amazed her how natural it would have been to add the word Sir. Not just natural, but right.

He slid the paper across the conference room table towards her. "I miss you, Maggie."

She froze.

"It's probably better this way," he said.

"Is it?" She could hardly force the words past the lump in her throat. "It's not for me."

"I'm a demanding bastard. I require any sub of mine to be honest and respectful at all times."

"A submissive. Is that what I was to you?"

"I was hoping so. I thought we were moving that direction. Clearly it was not what you wanted."

She lowered her hands to her lap so he couldn't see the way she was wringing them together beneath the table. The wall that faced the hallway was made of glass, so anyone passing by could see inside the room. This wasn't where she would have chosen to have this discussion, where anyone could witness her humiliation, but she didn't want to lose the opportunity. "It is what I want," she confessed, voice raw. "I was out of line in more ways than one." She took a breath, and he didn't speak. Unsure if she'd have another chance to apologise, she continued, "You own the company, and I should have told you what I had done. I called your phone that day, but I could have, *should have*, left a message. Regardless, the relationship we have — or had — outside of the office demanded I show you more respect." She blinked. "I'm not sure how to make it up to you, or if I can earn your forgiveness."

He pressed his palms together in front of his face and tapped his index fingers.

The moment drew out over at least thirty excruciating seconds before he spoke.

"I want to be very clear about a few things. First, your immediate action saved the Hoskins Group account. Second, I see that you made systems changes to ensure it doesn't occur again. I'm not happy the fuck-up happened to begin with, and I'm not happy we extended the term of the original agreement without giving the renewal due consideration."

She absently picked at a cuticle.

"Where I take exception to your behaviour is with your deviousness."

Maggie exhaled a shaky breath.

"You are supposed to be my most trusted adviser, Maggie. Is there another word that applies better? Distrustfulness, perhaps?"

That was worse. "No, Sir," she said.

"Where do you want to go from here?" he asked, dropping his hands and leaning towards her.

From the corner of her eye, she saw Barb walk by.

"I've been lonely, Mr Tomlinson." And the nightmares were a constant companion. "I'd like a second chance. I'm not sure I will ever be a perfect submissive. But I do know the time with you makes me want to try."

"Your behaviour would have to be punished." He leant back in his chair, studying her.

Oh God. Panic made her freeze. "Sir?"

"We discussed punitive spankings, Maggie. As I recall, you said you would not like to receive one. I promise, you would hate it."

She shuddered.

"I've taken some time to consider the situation from your point of view and understand why you would betray my confidence in that way."

Betray. Another harsh word.

He'd said he'd taken time to think about her motivations. Now she also saw things from his vantage. He'd been relentless in his honesty throughout and she understood how she'd hurt him. The knowledge made her heart ache.

"We could be good together, Maggie, on a personal as well as professional level. The decision as to whether we will be or not has always been in your hands. It still is."

"But I'd have to submit to your punishment."

"It's for you, as much as for me."

"I don't understand."

"You said you didn't know how to make it up. You can, anytime you want, by submitting to my cane."

"Jesus." Her heart slammed to a stop as fear collided with nerves.

"Five strokes. In my office. Your behaviour happened here, it will be punished here."

She couldn't string two coherent thoughts together, and speech became impossible. He gave her time to process what he'd said. "You... Are you serious?"

"Deadly."

His lips were set in a firm line. His eyebrows were relaxed, his shoulders loose. He was calm about this. And, she was certain, not negotiable. "I need to think."

"Of course."

* * * *

She spent the next day doing nothing but that. On Sunday, she went over to Vanessa's house.

Vanessa blended up an extra-large batch of margaritas and poured each of them a glass before they went outside to sit on the deck. Even that reminded her of being with David. "Bring Mama V up to date."

"Mama V?"

"One of the twins calls me that."

"Shit. They're twins?"

"Fraternal."

"And you're the Domme now?"

"Not always. But it turns out I look pretty good in boots and holding a whip."

"I bet you do." Maggie took a drink.

"Let me know if you'd like me to practise on you. I can show you a few tricks to get your man to lick your boots."

Maggie choked on a piece of ice. Vanessa laughed and slapped her on the back.

"Now get serious," Vanessa said. "And give me the ugly details."

Maggie brought her friend up to date, leaving nothing out. "And he wants me to call him Master."

"What the hell did you expect? Unlike my boys, your man's a Dom. It's not just a term of respect, it's an acknowledgement of the power exchange. And you get to decide whether you want to have that kind of relationship or flip him the bird. You get that, right? He didn't fire your ass, and you can continue your work relationship on professional terms. What the man asked you is if you wanted to be his sub. Do you?"

"It's not that easy."

"No relationship is, especially with someone as demanding as he is. Nothing comes with guarantees, you know that. Is it better to go for it or live with the regret?"

Maggie thought about her father's premature death. Would her mother have been better off if she'd never met him, sparing her the grief of loss?

"I'd trade in the twins for a chance like you've got," Vanessa said.

"Seriously?"

Vanessa drained her margarita in a single, big gulp. "Well, I'd consider it, at least. My advice? Call him what he wants and take your punishment like a big girl." She put down her empty glass. "I'll be back with the pitcher."

They spent the rest of the afternoon talking about a dozen different things, and by the time Maggie arrived back home, she felt settled in a way she hadn't before. She thought about sending him a text message then opted to wait.

That night, she had her usual, middle-of-the-night glass of water on the patio.

She looked at the cloudless sky and realised all the nightmares had one thing in common—they were trying to force her to look deep inside herself, to see what she feared then face it.

Alone, she did.

Yes, he might be dominating and overbearing, demanding more from her than she'd ever given. But he also gave more than she'd ever received—comfort, belief, trust. Next to him, all other relationships became insignificant. What he was offering was something real and authentic. There'd be no hiding, no other men, no lies or half-truths. She'd be physically exposed and emotionally vulnerable.

Was she brave enough to meet his demands?

At the office, he continued to be cool and polite. He didn't bring up their personal relationship. He seemed energetic and as focused as always, and that annoyed her. She envied his calm, wanting him to be as torn up inside as she was.

Over the next couple of days, she ran through the gamut of emotions before facing the truth. Somewhere along the line, she'd fallen in love with him. She admired his business acumen, but most of all she liked the way he was relentless in insisting she give everything she had to offer. She respected his inflexibility, his honesty, the way he cared for her when they were together. He made her feel safe and kept nightmares at bay.

Last week he'd said he missed her, taking the first step in repairing the damage she'd caused. She missed him and wanted to be with him, even if it meant she had to accept a caning as well as his terms.

On all levels, she was terrified.

During her lunch hour, she sent him a message asking if she could have a moment of his time late this afternoon.

He responded that he would see her at six o'clock.

Because she was dreading their meeting and had no idea what she was going to say or how she was going to approach him, the hours passed like minutes. By four-thirty, many of the employees had left. By five, she and David were the only two people in the building.

She tried to compose a letter, but couldn't put the words in the right order. A couple of minutes before their appointment, her cell phone alarm rang. As if there had been any possibility she wouldn't notice the time.

Maggie double-checked that the front door was secure and all office lights and equipment were turned off. At the top of the hour, she paused outside his door to drink in several breaths. Her body felt oxygen deprived, making her lightheaded. Then she knocked.

"Come in."

She closed the door behind her but stood there, waiting for his instructions, still unsure how to act. Bend over the desk? Lift her skirt? Remove it?

"Have a seat, Maggie." When she perched on the edge of the chair, he asked, "You wanted to see me?"

Of course he wasn't going to make this easy. Then again, he hadn't been privy to her thoughts and had no idea what she was going to say. "I came to ask if you'll forgive my behaviour."

He braced his elbows on the arms of his chair and linked his fingers together, appearing at ease.

"I've been thinking about our last conversation..." She was stumbling around and she hated it. After brushing her hair back from her face, she met his gaze. "What I mean is, damn it, Mr Tomlinson, I want to be with you. I accept your punishment and hope I can earn your forgiveness."

"You're certain you know what you're offering?"

"To get my butt blistered," she said wryly. "Mr Tomlinson."

"And after that?"

"To be in a relationship with you" — she looked down, then back up — "as your submissive."

He nodded, not betraying his inner thoughts. Damn, he was not the man she'd spent a weekend with. At his house, although he'd set the rules, he'd been gentler, encouraging, even teasing. "To be clear, my punishment is meant to reinforce the behaviour I expect from you. It's not because I am angry, it's because you were willingly and wilfully disobedient."

"Yes, Mr Tomlinson."

"I know we discussed the fact that I would use separation as a way to punish you, but that doesn't seem appropriate atonement in this case."

"I've already been separated, and it hurt," she admitted.

"Hurt us both," he said.

"I agree, Sir, that I still need to make amends." Her stomach plummeted with her words.

"I would normally administer ten stripes, but for two reasons, I decided on five. First of all, you've never been punished by me. And secondly, you were frank when I asked if you'd had any intention of telling me about the Hoskins deal."

"Thank you, Sir."

"I have no expectations that you will properly comport yourself. You can take as long as you want between stripes, and I will wait for you to get back into position before administering the next one. Your safe word stops it, and you go home alone. You can use 'eclipse' as many times as you need to. I have all night."

The temperature in the room was frigid, chilled by the coldness in his eyes. She ached to have him look at her with tenderness again. "I understand, Mr Tomlinson."

He stood and shrugged out of his suit jacket. She watched, fascinated, as he draped it over the back of his chair. He unfastened his cufflinks and dropped them. A sense of foreboding descended over her as they clinked together then thudded onto the gleaming desktop. She didn't blink as he rolled back his sleeves, exposing his forearms.

"I have a cane in my coat closet. Please fetch it."

His tone, his actions, his command, made the world slow down. He'd inexorably placed her in a submissive frame of mind where nothing existed but the two of them, and pleasing him. At its base, it was that simple. And Mr Tomlinson didn't demand more than he first offered.

Her knees wobbled as she rose to get the long, thin rattan.

He extended his hand and she cast her gaze at the floor as she offered it to him.

"Clear off my desk," he instructed. "You can put the items on the credenza, and close the blinds while you're there."

She did as he instructed, moving aside the stress balls she was tempted to squeeze, then turned to see him test the cane in the air. Its sound rent the air and chilled her. No way could she endure five cuts from that horrible thing.

"Plenty of subs have managed through history," he told her as if reading her mind. He placed the cane on the desk then closed and locked his office door.

"Strip."

The order surprised her. She'd expected to lift, even remove, her skirt, but hadn't anticipated he'd want her naked.

Her hands trembled as she removed her clothing, and she half-expected he'd help her undress. Instead, he watched her with a predatory gleam.

She left her clothing in a pile on the credenza while he moved aside the visitor chairs.

"On the desk," he told her.

Being bent over it would enable her to take it easier, and no doubt he'd reached the same conclusion.

He didn't offer her a hand, making it clear it was her choice at every point.

Once she was in position, vulnerable, she trembled. His tone of voice was so very distant, and she felt lost and alone.

"Ask me to punish you."

She looked back at him. The starkness on his face stunned her. His eyebrows were set in a narrow, resolved line. His chin jutted — there appeared to be no joy in this for him. And that pleased her. When he'd beaten her before, he'd appeared determined, but it had been softened by his intent to please and satisfy her.

Maggie took comfort from his features. It was as if they were in this together. Neither of them wanted this, but they both understood it was necessary. "I promise to be more honest with you in future, Sir. Please, Master David, punish me."

Their gazes met.

"Christ, Maggie. Do you know what you said?"

"I acknowledged you as my Master, Mr Tomlinson."

"I'm honoured," he told her. "Thank you for that. But it won't make this easier on you."

"I suspected as much, Master." She grabbed hold of the far end of the desk. But that didn't help. The first stripe landed on her buttocks, ricocheting through her body, making her scream and lose her grip. *Fuck.* She'd never felt anything like that before. Tears filled her eyes.

She had no idea how long it took her to get back in position, but there was no doubt of the effectiveness of his cane.

Master Tomlinson struck her again, and agony tore her from the inside out.

She fought and struggled to right herself, telling herself over and over that she was almost halfway through.

He didn't speak to her as he placed the third below her buttocks.

She fell forward, sobbing. She curled up into herself, knowing this was the first time she'd cried. He'd told her he'd have her in tears, and Master Damien had warned her as well. They'd all assumed it would be because of the beating. But it wasn't. She was shattered by the emotional wedge that had been between them, devastated by his distance even now. She'd never liked to be pampered and cuddled, and now she needed it, needed *him*.

He picked her up from the desk, carried her to a chair and held her while she sobbed. She felt as if she'd kept herself in a shell her whole life, refusing to experience everything it had to offer. And if she wanted to be with David, he wouldn't allow her that luxury.

David stroked her hair and soothed her.

She appreciated the fact he cared about her enough to demand she meet him where he was, holding nothing back. She settled against him. This was the first time he'd touched her since he'd confronted her about her transgression. She never wanted to go this long without his tenderness again.

Minutes dragged and shadows lengthened before she pulled back and said, "Can we get it over with?"

"You can continue another day."

"Please, no." He'd never let her shirk her duties, and having the remainder of the punishment looming in front of her would consume her thoughts. "I'm ready."

"You're certain?"

She didn't want to leave the comfort of his chest, the protection of his arms. "Yes, Master."

Maggie made her way to the desk. Its surface was marred by her tears and sweat. She feared it would be worse when they were finished.

Now that he'd done his worst, broken her down, and shown her what to expect, she could manage the rest.

This one caught her thighs and she sobbed, but didn't scream, surrendering to the agony instead of fighting it. When they'd talked about a punishment spanking, she'd told him it would be difficult for her because her Dom would be distant and remote. That wasn't the case. She knew this deepened what they shared. The way he'd cradled her had nurtured her. This lesson, she'd never forget, even though it wasn't the one he'd intended to deliver.

More than anything, she wanted things to be the way they had been at his house.

This was a means to make that happen. In that regard, she looked forward to having it over.

"Last one," he told her when she offered herself to him.

He seared her, and before she'd absorbed the impact, he was there, sitting on the desk, gathering her close. "Maggie mine."

She'd wondered if she'd hear those words again.

He kissed her forehead and swiped away her tears. "We'll go to your place," he said. "I'll drive you in your car. Mine should be safe enough in the parking garage."

David moved her to a chair and bundled her lingerie into her purse as he searched for her keys. He helped her back into her shoes, skirt and blouse then said, "Stay here."

Five minutes later, he was illegally parked in front of the building and helping her outside into the car.

She barely remembered the drive home, or the shower, or him dabbing the bruise cream onto her skin before holding her beneath the covers.

When the shock wore off, he was looking down at her. "I love you, Maggie mine," he told her.

"You..."

"Yeah." He stroked her forehead. "I love you. I've missed you so much."

"Oh, Master."

"Mr Tomlinson is fine, I've decided," he said.

"Really?"

"You're right, it's ours. Though, from time-to-time, you're welcome to call me Master."

"Will you do me a favour, Mr Tomlinson?"

"Anything."

"Fuck me? I can't bear it if you don't."

"You're up for it?"

"Fucking fuck me, Master."

"Well, since you asked so nice." He left the bed long enough to grab a condom from his wallet and something from her drawer. He cuffed her hands above her head then moved between her legs, cockhead poised to enter her pussy and said, "Tell me you love me, Maggie."

"It took me a while to figure it out, but I did, yesterday. I love you, Mr Tomlinson."

He claimed her mouth and demanded her surrender as he plunged into her cunt. He reached up and closed one hand around the cuffs, bringing them even closer.

His thrust spoke of desperation, of claiming, of marking, and she wanted all that and more.

Ending the kiss, he said, "Mine, Maggie."

"Yours, Master," she replied with softness and surrender.

"You're moving in with me."

"Is that a request?"

He drove into her. She lifted her hips and wrapped her legs around his waist.

"What do you think?"

She laughed. "I think you're non-negotiable."

"Not true."

It was all she could do to keep her gaze focused on him when she wanted to close her eyes and surrender to the moment. But that would mean sealing out the sight of him with his revealingly blue eyes, dark hair and intense features. "Not true, Mr Tomlinson?"

"I'm persuasive. I know you won't be coerced, and your mind may be willing to resist me, but your flesh can be convinced."

"Is that right?" She loved this more temperate side of him. It made him richer and more complex.

"Sunday morning lattes," he said.

"That's unfair."

He slowly pumped inside her, filling her up.

"Hot tub for two."

"Hmm..."

"The freedom to scream as long and as loud as you like. Floggings, spankings, orgasms so powerful you can't walk the next day."

"Master is trying for an unfair advantage."

"Any advantage," he corrected. "And I cook dinner."

"Okay, you win. I'll pack my bags."

"Bring your damn corset and the rest of your lingerie and toys."

"All of them?"

"All of them," he affirmed. "And we'll also need some time to rework your employment contract."

Even though he was in her, she froze. "Sir?"

"I want you as a partner, an equal. I want you to stay because you want to stay."

If her heart hadn't been melting before, it would be now. He continued his rhythmic movement, mere inches from her face. This was the kind of intimate conversation she could get used to. But there was one thing bothering her. "My mother, Mr Tomlinson?"

"Needs a good caning herself."

She laughed, and that made her pussy tighten.

"She'll get her bonus, but it will come from her efforts, not yours. She succeeds or fails on her own merits. Fair?"

Habit made her want to protest, but she kept her mouth shut. He was not only being equitable, he was being more than fair.

"Agreed, Maggie?"

"Yes, Master."

He grinned and pulled out all the way before plunging back in.

"I love the way your ginormous cock feels, Sir."

"Ginormous?"

"Extraordinarily so."

He fucked her to completion, making sure she came before he did, always, *always* taking care of her.

"One more thing, you'll always be in my heart as well as my cuffs."

"Mr Tomlinson, Master, there's no place I'd rather be."

MASTERED

Sierra Cartwright

What you see isn't
what you get...

FOR THE
SUB

Mastered: For the Sub

Sierra Cartwright

Released November 2013

Excerpt

Chapter One

"Another drink, Sir?"

Startled out of his reverie by the softness of a woman's voice, Niles looked over the rim of his empty glass. Brandy, one of the house's submissives, stood in front of him, her legs close together, her shoulders pulled back in a sexy way that thrust her chest forward.

Had he been so lost in thought that he hadn't heard her approach? Or were her movements so graceful and perfect that she'd managed to silently cross the Den's patio?

Given her seductively high stilettos, he doubted the latter.

Her long blonde hair flowed over her shoulders and down her back. Tonight she wore a short, slinky black dress that covered everything, but seemed more intriguing because of it. The material clung to her, highlighting her ample breasts, trim waist and curvy bottom. This woman—sub—appealed to every one of his masculine sensibilities.

Her legs were bare, and her black heels emphasised the feminine shape of her ankles. For a moment, he fantasised about placing her on her back, removing her shoes then stroking his fingers against her instep before applying a cane to the soles of her feet.

He shook his head to banish the image.

It had been years since he'd played with a woman in anything other than a detached way. In fact, it hadn't happened since the tragic death of his beautiful, accomplished wife and sub, Eleanor.

But right now, he was thinking about touching Brandy in a way meant for their mutual satisfaction.

"Sir?" she asked, tipping her head. "Master Niles?"

The motion swept her hair to the side, snaring his interest. The locks were long enough, he mused, to be used as part of a hot bondage scene.

"Would you prefer to be alone, Sir?"

"Actually, no." The answer surprised him.

A month ago, he'd declined the invitation to tonight's party. Every fall, Master Damien hosted a get-together for Doms and Dommes who had been members of the Den for at least seven years. It was a small, select group, and they gathered to play poker, sip the finest single malt on the planet, enjoy conversation, and if they chose, scene with house subs. Not many people availed themselves of the playrooms, however, as most were in relationships, and this exclusive gathering focused on socialising, which was not his long suit.

Damien had pestered Niles to the point of annoyance.

Despite his reluctance, and tired of his own company after spending a week at home by himself, Niles had acquiesced.

But after half an hour of mindless white lies, assuring his friends and acquaintances that he was well, he'd made his escape to the solitude of the patio. He'd dragged a chair close to the crackling fire pit to enjoy the sunset. Today had been a mild day, and summer was breathing her last gasps before surrendering to the inevitable shorter, colder, bleaker days.

Brandy, a natural submissive, rather than one who'd been trained for it, cast her gaze down at the ground before looking up him. "I never said thank you for what happened at the last Ladies' Night."

"No thanks necessary," he assured her. "Any Dom would have done the same thing."

Many times, there was an assumption among new Doms that subs wearing the house's purple wristband welcomed any attention. A first-time visitor had made that error with Brandy.

Master Damien had not served alcoholic beverages at Ladies' Night, opting for frou-frou, sugar-laced umbrella drinks that the ladies seemed to like. But that hadn't stopped the guest from drinking before he arrived.

Even when Brandy had used the Den's safe word, the asshole had continued on, forcing her to her knees and shoving his dick in his mouth. Niles had noticed her distress and stepped in.

Truthfully he'd enjoyed throwing the wannabe Dom out the front door. The physical altercation had dissipated some of the angst churning in his gut, emotion he couldn't get rid of otherwise. If Master Damien or anyone else had noticed the uppercut Niles had delivered to the guy's jaw, no one had mentioned it.

Seeing his bruised knuckles the next day had been satisfying, but not as rewarding as seeing the current, exquisite expression of gratitude on Brandy's face.

He rolled the empty glass between his palms, keeping his hands busy so he didn't yield to the temptation to reach out and touch her.

Niles realised he knew little about her. He'd seen her around the Den for years. She was always unfailingly obedient, but she didn't stand out. No wonder Damien continued to have her at his events.

"If you'd like to go to one of the private rooms, Sir, I'm available."

His cock hardened. He met her gaze. Her blue eyes were wide open and she gave him a quick smile that slammed his solar plexus. *Fuck.* Why had he never noticed how attractive she was? Maybe because she wasn't the type he usually went for.

At six feet tall, his wife had looked him in the eye when she had donned the heels he liked. She'd been runway-model thin, with deep brown eyes and raven hair styled in a sleek, no-nonsense bob.

The two women couldn't be any more different.

Suddenly, though, the idea of bending Brandy over, making her scream his name as she came, appealed to every dominant urge. Still, he didn't want to scene just because she had a misplaced sense of gratitude. "You owe me nothing."

"I think you misunderstood. It was an invitation, Sir." She linked her hands at her back.

Interesting. Brandy was well trained, a perfect sub. And if he wasn't mistaken, she'd tucked her hands out of sight so he couldn't see the way she was fidgeting.

"I'm afraid I was being bold," she said, still looking at the ground.

So she was nervous, and he understood why. Though she was often summoned to the dungeon, he was certain she initiated few, if any, of the scenes. "I respect a woman who asks for what she wants."

As he stood, he put down his glass. Brandy didn't glance up. He placed his forefinger beneath her chin and tipped her head back.

She smelt of cinnamon with a tangy undercurrent of arousal. The spicy scent intrigued him. He'd expected something more floral, in keeping with her femininity. For the first time since Eleanor had passed, he wanted to scene for pleasure. "I accept," he said.

Brandy smiled.

The slow, sensuous curve of her lips made something deep inside start to melt. "After you," he said.

She scooped up his glass and started towards the main house. Her hips swayed from side to side, not in an exaggerated movement, but with natural feminine grace. He was looking forward to getting her naked.

Responding to a male instinct as old as time, he placed his fingers against the small of her back.

Gregorio, the Den's caretaker, opened the patio doors for them.

"We'll be availing ourselves of one of the playrooms," Niles said.

Gregorio drew his dark eyebrows together. Obviously, he hadn't been expecting that news.

"Let me know if you need anything," Gregorio said. "You as well," he said to Brandy as he accepted the glass from her.

"I'll take good care of her," Niles promised.

"See that you do," Gregorio said.

He appreciated the way Master Damien and Gregorio ensured everyone's safety, but this time it rankled. Niles would do nothing to harm Brandy.

With a nod towards the watchful Gregorio, Niles guided her through the kitchen then down the stairs that led to Damien's elaborate dungeon.

Niles owned a production company that often filmed at the Den, and he'd appeared in a number of their videos. He knew the rooms well, all the apparatus that was available and each of the implements he could apply to her body.

He stopped at the bar and snagged two bottles of water before asking Brandy if she had any preference on which room to enter.

"Sir?"

Clearly she expected him to make the decisions. Under normal circumstances, he would. But this evening was anything but ordinary. "This was your idea," he told her. "So I'm betting you have an idea or two about what you'd like to have happen."

"In that case, Sir, first door on the right."

He nodded, pleased with her answer. Because of its sparseness, this was one of his favourite playrooms. A hook hung from the ceiling, and a chair stood off to one side, tucked beneath a padded bench. The far wall was dominated by crops, whips, floggers and a tawse handcrafted by Master Marcus. As with all the rooms, there was a small sink and counter, and a cupboard stocked with necessities, including wipes, lube, condoms and towels.

She entered ahead of him. He paused to seal them in relative privacy. At the Den, all rooms had a window cut into the door. Every interaction was observed by Gregorio or Master Damien, meaning there was no such thing as complete seclusion, a policy Niles endorsed.

When he turned, he saw her kneeling in the middle of the room, head bowed, hands on her thighs. The subs—male and female—that he professionally dominated were actors and models. Each act was scripted and choreographed, and each response was exploited to ensure maximum effect. Screaming, whimpering and begging were all expected from the participants—after all, no one wanted to pay money for a download in which the spankee was silent.

He was reminded that Brandy, too, submitted for a living, but there were no cameras, directors or second takes. This was between two willing participants for no reason other than pleasure. "Stand, please," he said. "Hands over your head."

Niles drew her dress up, exposing her beautiful body, inch by perfect inch.

She wore a scrap of material that served as panties. And she had on a black shelf bra that lifted her breasts. "I'm a fortunate man tonight, Brandy."

"Thank you, Sir."

He offered her the dress. "Fold it and put it on the counter then return to me."

Wordlessly, she did as instructed. She stood in front of him, her legs spread slightly and her hands looped behind her back. He noticed the telltale rapid rise and fall of her chest, indicating she was not as relaxed as she appeared.

It might have been ego, but he liked to think that this might mean something to her. If it didn't, he could live with that. Passing an hour or two together would make the evening more pleasant than he'd anticipated. "How expensive are your panties?"

"Very," she said.

"Sorry in advance."

"Occupational hazard, Sir."

He crossed to one of the drawers and took out a pair of safety scissors. Almost every week, he cut the material from an actress. This, however, was different. She wouldn't be turning in an expense report for replacement lingerie. Well, not to his company.

She stood still as he slid the blunted end between her skin and lace. "Ask me to do it."

Brandy met his gaze. "Do it," she said. "Cut the panties off me, Sir."

He did. The useless scrap pooled to the floor. "I like a shaved pussy," he told her.

"I'm pleased you approve, Sir."

She'd given him a stock answer. Any sub, any time would reply with a variation of those words. From what he'd observed, her training had been complete, exquisite even. But something in the pit of his stomach yearned for more—demanded more—from her. Honesty. He wanted honesty.

Maybe, he told himself, this was the real her. But part of him wondered if she was different away from the Den.

Stupidly, belatedly, he looked at her left hand. No ring adored her fingers, not that that meant anything. "Remove your bra and drop it."

Without hesitation, she did so.

The room was silent, save the sound of his heartbeat and her shallow breaths. "Look at me and tell me what you want, pretty sub."

Their gazes collided.

"To please you," she said.

"Then stop with the expected bullshit."

She gasped. "I'm not sure what you mean, Master Niles."

"I think you do."

Over the course of several seconds, she licked her upper lip.

"Stalling?" he asked.

"No, Sir. I'm trying to figure you out," she replied.

"That might be the most truthful thing you've said yet."

"You're a Dom, a very experienced one." She took her time, making every word count. "I'm a sub."

"Is that why you approached me? Do you want me to treat you as if you're interchangeable with any actress on the planet? I assure you, I don't see you that way."

To her credit, she took her time in answering. He liked that she was deliberate.

"No. It's not."

"I don't have a script, Brandy. And if I did, I wouldn't follow it. I would rather you be real with me, and natural. I need you to open up." With the power of his will, he held her gaze captive. "I need to know about your limits, but even more, I want to know the things that quicken your pulse and the sensations that make you writhe in ecstasy. I demand your participation, but not your blind obedience. Those are my terms."

"You'll think I'm selfish."

"I'm willing to take the risk."

"In that case, Sir, I love any kind of flogging, but especially one on my pussy, followed by a long, hard fuck."

His cock throbbed at the passion in her words. When he orchestrated a shoot, he never had sex with the actors. He'd bring them off manually or with a toy, but he kept his dick in his pants. Over the years, that had added to his mystique. He wasn't interested in his reputation. He had one purpose—grow the company's revenues.

"The truth is, if you get into what we're doing, I get off." She paused and sighed, as if either trying to figure it out for herself or find words to explain what she meant to him. "The energy builds on itself." Her blue eyes lightened, radiating her inner enthusiasm. "I can scene with almost anyone and enjoy it as long as they do, too. I love my work at the Den."

Niles had underestimated her earlier. He'd figured Damien continued to have her at his events because she pleased his guests and didn't stand out, but she was more complex than that. Early in his business career, Niles had learnt that any employee with a genuine desire to please should be rewarded and retained. Damien had apparently reached the same conclusion, after all, even during times of economic hardship, the Den's membership had continued to grow, despite some hefty membership fees. "I'd be delighted to redden your cunt," he told her.

"Thank you, Sir."

Even though the answer was rote, her tone conveyed gratitude. He left her long enough to grab a pair of cuffs and to lower the hook. Without being told, she extended her arms. As he fastened the soft fabric around her wrists, he asked, "Do you want to use anything other than the club's safe word?"

"Halt is fine, Sir."

"Any slow word?"

"I can't imagine one will be necessary, Sir."

Niles was adept at pushing subs to the utmost limits. After all, that created the most compelling of all videos. But he also knew how to read a sub's non-verbal clues. He knew, oftentimes before they did, when they'd had enough. "Do you have any conditions or limits I need to be aware of?"

"I have no medical concerns. As far as limits, nothing that will leave a permanent scar."

He nodded and affixed the cuffs to the metal hook. "If at any time you're too uncomfortable, let me know," he said.

"Of course, Sir."

"Do you need a spreader bar for your legs?"

"That won't be necessary, Master Niles."

He knew she'd do anything he commanded, but he wanted her to be able to let go and surrender to his lash. "Would it make the experience more pleasant?"

"Yes, Sir."

Already he was learning to look at her eyes for an answer. The depths were expressive and revealed more than her words and tone together. He saw her gratitude and anticipation. She was looking forward to this. He wondered if she often had the chance to just let go and enjoy herself. Since this was her job, it was her obligation to ensure the Den's guests had their needs met. Tonight, he wanted more than that for her. He was glad she'd approached him, rather than wait for another Dom to claim her.

Niles fetched a metal bar. As he knelt, she widened her stance to allow him to attach the straps to her ankles.

This close to her, he inhaled the unmistakable, sharp scent of female arousal. Unable to resist, he parted her labia. "You're already damp, pretty sub."

"Yes, Sir," she whispered.

He slipped a finger inside her hot pussy. She locked her knees. "It's okay to respond. In fact, I'd like it."

He pressed his thumb to her clit then pulled back.

"Nice, Sir."

He alternated between applying intense pressure and a glancing touch, keeping her off guard. She swayed in time to his fingering and the way he teased her clit.

"I'm getting wetter, Sir."

He backed off a bit. "Are you close to coming?"

"Yes, Master Niles."

Nothing surprised him. He'd been with women who could orgasm from the lightest of touches. Others were capable of multiple orgasms. There were some who required so much stimulation that he was grateful for the assistance of an electric vibrator. Each sub was unique, and he enjoyed finding the right combination of touches that would make her respond.

"Should I get you off?"

"It's your choice, Sir."

"Of course it is." He slid his finger deeper before pulling out. With a rhythmic, rocking motion, he increased the frequency of his thrusts.

She whimpered.

So, damn hot. Her pussy tightened around his finger and she moved as much as the bar permitted, encouraging him to put more pressure on her clit. Wanting to please her, he followed her lead.

"I'd like to come, Sir."

"I'm sure you would," he said in soothing tones at odds with the way he stimulated her.

Her whimpers became groans.

"Sir, I'm going to come."

"Not yet, you're not."

"Master Niles, I'm begging you to either let me come, or stop now, Sir. At least"—she dragged in a couple of rapid breaths—"slow down."

Ignoring her, he continued the relentless torment.

"Damn, Sir…"

Her beautiful walls all but convulsed around his finger. How was it he'd never scened with her before?

"This is a taste of what's to come, sub," he warned. He moved his hand to sting her pussy with a quick, vicious slap.

She called out his name and jerked her hips as she came.

He reached to put one hand behind her and another on her abdomen, steadying her. She was so far gone, trembling and moaning, that he wasn't sure she'd be able to keep her balance otherwise. He hadn't pulled the hook taut, so it offered little support.

Niles smiled. "You're so perfect, Brandy." He looked up at her. A fine sheen of perspiration dotted her chest, and she took a deep breath.

When she appeared to have herself under control she said, "I came without permission, Sir."

Like she had earlier, she tilted her head to one side. Rather than drawing her eyebrows together when she was puzzled, she angled her head. How long would it be until he knew all her responses? "Now I have a reason to punish you when I see you again," he said.

"Punish?" she echoed. "You're a fiend, Sir."

"Let's add disrespect to the list, shall we?" he mused.

"But, Sir—"

"Along with arguing."

"I..." She closed her mouth.

"Good choice."

Her head was still tilted, and he doubted he'd ever seen anything more charming. And he wasn't finished with her yet. "Your pussy is bright red," he said.

"It feels as if it's on fire, Sir. And that was from a single smack."

She sounded as if she were looking forward to more.

"Did you like it?"

"Mmm."

"I've heard that sound when women eat chocolate cake."

"That, Sir, was better than cake. Even though I wasn't supposed to come —"

"Oh, I meant for that to happen, I assure you."

She was silent a moment before adding, "Thank you, Sir."

He placed his hands so that both were on her rear then moved his face between her legs. "Fuck my face, pretty sub."

Brandy was too well trained to question him or hesitate.

Instead she moved her hips.

He parted her buttocks and pressed his thumbs against her anal whorl, all the while keeping her from moving backwards.

"Dear God, Master Niles..."

He liked the high pitch to her voice, as if her vocal cords were rubbed raw by desire. After easing one thumb a bit deeper in her ass, he sucked her clit into his mouth then released her to cover her pussy with long sweeps of his tongue. He liked the musky taste of her and the urgency of her responses. If she wasn't restrained, he had no doubt she'd dig her hands in his hair and hold his head prisoner. As it was, she had to count on him to support her weight as she ground her cunt against his mouth.

Her heat covered his face.

"Do me," she demanded.

Fuck. This woman was hot.

It had been so long since he'd felt this alive, this engaged, that he'd go a long way to please her.

He used his tongue as she moved her hips. She bent her knees to change the angle as much as possible and give him greater access. He slid his tongue into her dampness and she screamed.

"I can't hold off, Sir!"

In response, he forced his thumb all the way inside her tightest hole. She continued to press her pelvis forward, and he dug the fingers of his left hand into the soft flesh of her buttocks.

Without another warning, her body went rigid before she moved again in short, desperate little motions as she fought for her orgasm.

With his mouth, his touch, he helped her along.

She raised herself onto her tiptoes, and the slight shift forced his tongue deeper.

One of her heels slammed onto the floor, a sound of satisfaction if he'd ever heard one.

"That was sensational," she whispered as he drew away. "Thank you, again."

An intense flare of lust gnawed at his insides. Making subs shatter was his passion. But it was nothing more than a job. He never engaged. Instead, he held himself and his emotions at a distance. He used a critical and artistic eye to make the scene sizzle. This time, though, his focus was solely on the curvaceous blonde. "I think that's enough of an appetiser."

"Oh, Sir..."

After washing up, he returned to her. He skimmed his forefinger across her cheekbone. "Would you like to continue?"

Instead of the usual response where she would defer to his decision, she said, "Yes, please."

The surety in her voice stoked his craving for her.

He crossed to the wall and raised the hook, stretching her body taut, keeping her in place and wide open for him. "Comfortable?" he asked as he crossed the room to check her bonds and positioning. He knew erotic pain could trump real cramps, at least in the short-term. It was his responsibility to ensure she was free to enjoy his torture.

He walked around her, looking at her from every angle. "You're a beautiful woman, Brandy."

Her nipples were erect, as if begging for his touch. There was nothing clinical about the way he took hold of each and squeezed the pink flesh between his thumbs and forefingers. This was about her pleasure rather than for maximum effect.

With a soft sigh, she closed her eyes.

"Look at me," he instructed.

She complied right away.

"Good," he told her. "As much as possible, I want you looking at me. Talk to me, communicate with me. Scream, even."

"I'm not much of a screamer, Sir."

"Yet," he countered.

"Challenge on, Sir."

"Bratty sub."

"You could have ordered me to be quiet."

"No chance in hell." He couldn't remember anything this pleasurable in...perhaps years. "Any preference in floggers?"

"Thuddy, not stingy."

"So I can beat you for a good, long time?"

"Yes, please, Sir."

"It will be my pleasure."

Her eyes were wide. He saw expectancy in the deep blue depths. He and Brandy were more alike than he might have thought. Like him, what they had done had merely whetted her appetite.

About the Author

Sierra Cartwright was born in Manchester, England and raised in Colorado. Moving to the United States was nothing like her young imagination had concocted. She expected to see cowboys everywhere, and a covered wagon or two would have been really nice!

Now she writes novels as untamed as the Rockies, while spending a fair amount of time in Texas…where, it turns out, the Texas Rangers law officers don't ride horses to roundup the bad guys, or have six-shooters strapped to their sexy thighs as she expected. And she's yet to see a poster that says Wanted: Dead or Alive. (Can you tell she has a vivid imagination?)

Sierra wrote her first book at age nine, a fanfic episode of Star Trek when she was fifteen, and she completed her first romance novel at nineteen. She actually kissed William Shatner (Captain Kirk) on the cheek once, and she says that's her biggest claim to fame. Her adventure through the turmoil of trust has taught her that love is the greatest gift. Like her image of the Old West, her writing is untamed, and nothing is off-limits.

She invites you to take a walk on the wild side…but only if you dare.

Sierra Cartwright loves to hear from readers. You can find her contact information, website details and author profile page at http://www.total-e-bound.com.

Total-E-Bound Publishing

www.total-e-bound.com

Take a look at our exciting range of literagasmic™
erotic romance titles and discover pure quality
at Total-E-Bound.